Elephants ... Sky

Gerard Kelly

Edited by

Jean Kelly

Chapter One

Toni

"Mum I look totally stupid." The girl wasn't happy, "Everyone is in school is going to laugh at me."

"But I think you look so lovely!"

"Your idea of 'lovely!' seems to have gone utterly wrong! Just don't go there! I look ridiculous!"

Mum was lost for words.

"And tell me why do I have to have my hair tied back in this? Have I suddenly got nits or something?"

"Darling, you know that is how children dressed during the war; you have an important job to do at school today and you will have to look your best."

"If this is supposed to be my best I would hate to think what 'worst' might be. Everyone will be calling me a 'total loser' now!"

Toni gazed into the mirror. Her hair had been tied in a blue spotted head scarf to match the dress her mum had made for her. She hated the odd buttons down the front but when she complained that they didn't match, mum just retorted with,

"Oh, Toni! There is supposed to be a war on!" She refused to change anything.

Toni also had a hand knitted cardigan which her Nan had made for her. To be truly authentic, Nan had even gone to the bother of unravelling an old jumper of her own so it could be knitted up again. Toni didn't see the point. The cardigan felt awful, it was all stiff, like cardboard, it was scratchy; she would never wear it again – ever!

Toni put on her lucky necklace. It was made from a thin strip of leather long enough to go round her neck. It had a green pendant in the shape of an owl which had a hole through it so it could hang neatly in the middle.

Toni often had good luck when she wore it but she would have to be careful not to let her mother see it today. Mum didn't like her wearing anything round her neck when she went to school.
"Someone might make a grab for you and pull it. It would leave a nasty mark or even cut into your neck."
Mothers were always fussing; they didn't know anything.

Almund Street Primary School had a long history that went back as far as the 1930's. It was an old red brick building with several floors, connected by hard stone staircases that had been worn down by thousands of feet over the years.

There were once three entrances to Almund School. Each had 'Boys', 'Girls' or 'Infants' carved in a rough sandstone block above their doorways. Nowadays all the children came in through the same 'Infants' door, close to the school office.

Whenever there was an important historical date in the calendar, Almund Primary School was sure to put on a great show. They didn't need good reason to celebrate. Hardly a term went by when something wasn't highlighted.

Already this year the teachers had dressed as sailors in memory of the Battle of Trafalgar and even as 'Oompa Loompas' on Roald Dahl's birthday.

There was a well polished brass plaque in the assembly hall. It had been there for many years. It commemorated a tragedy which struck the school in 1942. On that particular day there had been a rare, daylight bombing raid over Portsmouth. During the raid one of the enemy planes overflew its target, getting lost in the English countryside. Discovering a single bomb remaining in the bay, they dropped it onto the ground below, not daring to risk trying to land back in Germany with a live bomb on board.

At precisely, 2:15 in the afternoon, all the children in Almund School (as it was then called), were packed into the school's air raid shelter. The lonesome bomb scored a direct hit, exploding right on top of the shelter and giving all the children below no chance of escape.

The tragedy sent a wave of pain and despair through the entire community. Hardly a household wasn't touched in some way by the catastrophe. The remembrance of the event soon became engraved forever into the town's memory.

The names of all the children, along with those of the teachers who had guided them to this place of 'safety', were recorded in a leather bound book which rested below, on a simple oak shelf.

Today all the children were going to re-live the event, dressing up in the correct clothes and carrying mock gas mask cases. At the exact time, they were going to run out onto the playground then sit directly above the spot where the air raid shelter had once been located. Benches from the school gym had been arranged in readiness. Then the names of all those in the leather book would be solemnly read out.

Toni was upset. Her judo lesson had been cancelled to allow the school hall to be used for their 'Second World War Tea-Party'; she would far rather have thrown her best friend around than be forced to eat 'spam'.

Lots of people had been invited. Adults who had once attended Almund Primary School were going to attend, along with veterans of the armed services and even the mayor was to put in an appearance.

There was to be a special war time menu. They could choose from: Spam fritters, Potato Jane, Woolton Pie, Baked beans on toast, Cheese pudding, Barley soup, Steam pudding and Carrot cake. Mr Cuthbert the head teacher wanted guests and children to sit together so the youngsters could ask questions and talk about what life had been like during the war.

Toni announced that she wasn't going to bother having anything to eat; the list was absolutely disgusting. If she was really hungry, she might just about chance the 'beans on toast'; at worst she would manage with just a glass of orange juice then come home for a proper, civilised tea in front of the TV.

Toni had a loud clear voice. A voice which was often heard reverberating round the class room, much to her poor teacher's annoyance, with this gift, she had naturally been chosen to be the one who would read out all of the names, during the special, commemorative two minutes of silence.

Toni held the lucky green owl in her hand. She needed all the good fortune she could find today if she was to get things right. Some of the names were real tongue twisters.

        Miss Agnes Atkin
        Miss Roberta Catrick
        Miss Edwina Shaum
        Miss Clementine Hodgness
        Edna Cawthorn,
        Nathaniel Blackledge
        Marjorie Turner
        Henrietta Cranton
        Wallace Burrage
        Eunice Woods....

It was a long list with many names.

"Why do the first ones in the list say Miss like 'Miss Agnes Atkin' while others just have their names?" Toni wondered.

Mum knew the answer to that question; she could remember it from when she had been in school herself.

"They were the teachers; Miss Agnes Atkin was the head teacher. That's why her name is first."

"So the head teacher was killed along with the others too; it's so sad. But why are there no men teachers in the school and how come none of the ladies were married?"

"I can remember being told that after the terrible bomb the Local Education Authority had to find a new head teacher to run the school. It wasn't easy; remember all the men teachers had gone off to fight in the war."

"What did they do then?"

"They had to bring in an experienced head teacher from one of the tiny village schools, someone who was used to running a school. It had to be a person who could cope in the difficult times the nation was going through."

"It must have been very difficult for her. One day she was in a comfortable village school, the next she was running a huge school with lots of children, right in the middle of the war."

Mum agreed, "I don't remember who she was, but she stayed as head teacher for many years until she retired. Her name will be in a special book somewhere in the school.

"What book is that?"

"When I was at school, the head teacher used to have the school's log book in his office. He let us see it once. He kept a kind of school diary in it. Though I do not know if they still have one nowadays."

Toni read through the long list again, this was not going to be easy.

She would have willingly swapped with her friend Izzy; all she had to do was to push Freddy round in his wheelchair. Billy Preston would be with his minder too.

Lessons for the day had a general Second World War theme. The children were learning what it must have been like to be a child in war time. They all had their own ration books to help them organise and plan food menus for their pretend families.

Toni's pretend family had three children all under ten years old. Her supposed husband was in the army driving a lorry somewhere in Scotland. Miranda naturally had only one child and her husband, as she kept telling everyone, was a pilot in the RAF.

Swimming lessons had been cancelled for the week. Mr Cuthbert explained children didn't go swimming during the war, besides the town only had an open air pool in the 1940's. One of her teachers claimed that when she had been at school, her class used to go swimming in the river in the summer time.
Toni wasn't a very good swimmer but she had been enjoying going to the pool for the last few weeks.

They had been learning about water safety, learning how to rescue someone from drowning and how to resuscitate a person who had been in the water for a long time. They had to take turns pretending to be drowning; Toni was good at the 'shouting for help' part, though Miranda pretended not to hear her.
They had learnt how to rescue each other, and then they had all practised giving 'the kiss of life' to a dummy on the side of the pool. If Toni had her way she would have wanted to rescue and resuscitate Niall Horon or Harry Styles. There was no way she was ever going to kiss Miranda!

Toni wasn't sure she would really be able to do it herself; if she ever came across someone in difficulty but the swimming coach thought it did not matter.

"If you know what to do, you would be able to give instructions to someone else, then you could help to save a life that way, even if you cannot do it yourself."

Toni could not imagine it ever happening. If she saw Miranda in the water she would have to phone her hairdresser first and then stand by with a makeup bag!

Almost all of Toni's class got dressed up for this special day. They had cardboard labels on their clothes just like evacuees had worn. Toni had to smile to herself because, for once, Tracey did not stand out from the rest of the class. They were all just as scruffy as she usually was.

Miranda wasn't happy either, her clothes were always immaculate, though her mother had ordered special 'replica evacuee clothes for her from eBay - sadly not in her beloved pink!

Mr Cuthbert, the head teacher, decided he would have to wear a dress for the day. They had to call him Miss Cuthbert. He told them that all the men would have been called up to fight for their country, so there would only be women in the school to teach the children while the men were away.

Toni's Mum had told her that not many married ladies worked as teachers. They were supposed to be at home: that was 'where a woman's place was'.

Toni thought he was going a bit too far, but Mr Cuthbert was always eager and ready to dress up to take part in any school event. The memory of his overweight orange Oompa Loompa still gave her horrid dreams.

The children had been learning some of the songs popular in 1940.
Toni didn't think much of the music, she thought being made to sing, 'Roll out the barrel!' was too much for her dignity.

No proper modern sweets were allowed as snacks, but some children decided they were going to bring in bags of cough sweets because children did actually have those during the war.

"I cannot go to school looking like this!" Toni was still insisting, "If I meet anyone on the way they will stare at me!"
"Do not worry! Dad said he would drop you off at school so you don't have to walk in the streets dressed like that."

"Drop me off! Oh no he won't! I don't want anyone to see me getting out of his filthy old van. Samira gets dropped off by her mum's Porsche. Bradley's dad has a brand new Lexus! You can just imagine what they will think when they see me climbing out of Dad's shed! Miranda and her friends will have a field day!"

Mum hung her head in her hands. 'What other people thought' was becoming more and more important to Toni in her last few years at Primary school. She only wore a school uniform once she had checked the labels to make sure her clothes had not been bought at Tesco's!

"Dad can drop you off round the corner then, where no one will see you, then you have only a short walk to go to get to school.

Toni reluctantly agreed, "Whatever, but if he waves and honks his stupid horn, I know I will die of embarrassment!"

"If you like I will sign the form saying you have to have a spoonful of cod liver oil at break time! Now stop complaining and enter into the spirit of it all!" Mum threatened.

Toni clutched her magic Owl under her cardigan, in all the morning arguments, Mum had not seen it. The owl had been her 'awesome treasure' for a long time, ever since she had found it, under a loose floorboard in her Granny's house.

Chapter Two
Upstairs

The children were trying to work quietly in their classroom, filling in a special worksheet their teacher had prepared for them. It was quite difficult though. Every so often, Mr. Cuthbert would appear in the classroom to ask a question. He was wearing a pink spotted dress with a long white apron. Thankfully it covered his white legs, but they could see his usual school shoes and, what was much worse, the low neckline showed a glimpse of his hairy chest! What little hair he had on his head was tied up in a head scarf. He looked as if he was about to do some spring cleaning.

Every time Mr Cuthbert came into the room he was greeted with howls of laughter from all the children. Their teacher was trying hard to keep her face straight but she was finding it was very difficult.

Mrs Johnson, Toni's teacher, who had to be called 'Miss Johnson' for the day, was wearing a similar dress, only hers came just below her knees. She had told the children that during the war ladies had not been able to buy silk stockings, so she had done what women did in those days. She had rubbed gravy browning into her legs and then used a pencil to mark in the 'seam' at the back. Toni thought it was silly. The pencil line was not straight it wobbled all over the back of her legs.

"Why did you do that?" One of the children asked, "There isn't a war on now, you can buy stockings in the shops."

"We are trying to make it as realistic as we can. We can't actually have bombs landing and exploding in the play ground but we are trying to get as close to life during the Second World War as we can," was the reply.

"It would be great if we could have a real bomb!" One of the boys shouted, but Mrs Johnson just gave him one of her withering looks.

Toni wasn't working on the worksheet she had been given. She was practising reading the names of the children who had been in the air raid shelter when the bomb exploded. The names were strange to her ears. They didn't sound like children; they were more like her Nan's friends. She didn't have anyone in her class called Maggie or Edna and there wasn't a single Eddie or Frank in the class either. She wondered what would happen if she added Miranda Herbet-Cawsthorn to the list too.

Toni was feeling bored, she had already read through the list about five times, it was getting tedious. It was time for a break. She put up her hand.

"Please Mrs Johnson, Oh sorry, 'Miss' Johnson, can I go to the toilet please?"

Mrs Johnson gave her a stern look,

"I don't want you running across the playground to the toilets Toni Braithwaite; make sure you walk all the way."

Toni looked puzzled: the girls toilets were at the bottom of the stairs.

"The toilets used to be on the far side of the playground," Patricia told her, "Mrs Johnson is pretending they still are!"

Toni shook her head; the sooner things got back to normal the better. 'Miss' Johnson would have them all running round the play ground in their vests and knickers if she had her way. She was taking all this authentic stuff a bit too far.

Toni got out of her seat and headed for the door. There was a large poster on the wall outside her class room proclaiming, 'Keep Calm and Carry On." She preferred the one she had seen in town, it read: "Keep Calm and eat Cake."

The corridor was silent; all the children were in their classrooms. There was no one working in the corridors. No groups working with one of the Learning Mentors or teaching assistants. Mr Cuthbert had explained even up to quite recently there had only been a single teacher to each class. Children were all taught together no one got any special attention.

Toni imagined having Billy Preston in the room all the time would have been terrible. If he wasn't swearing at the teachers he had to be restrained from attacking one of the boys. How did teachers cope with boys like him in the 1940's?

Mr Cuthbert had shown them a thick leather strap he had found in a dusty drawer when he first became the head teacher. The children couldn't begin to imagine what it was like to be punished so cruelly, though her Dad said he had been given it many times when he was at school. Perhaps Billy Preston would have worn out a strap all on his own!

Toni decided now she had escaped from her class she could go exploring. Normally, she wouldn't have dared to wander into a different part of the school. She would be bound to meet someone round every corner she turned. Today there was only silly Mr Cuthbert to avoid. He was enjoying being dressed as a woman, perhaps he secretly was a transvestite?

There was a flight of stairs that led up to part of the school which was no longer used. The number of children attending Almund primary school had dropped a lot in recent years so there were apparently quite a few large redundant classrooms upstairs. Toni had been up there once or twice to help carry down costumes and scenery for the nativity play. Upstairs was just a storage area now, it was quite definitely 'Out of Bounds'.

Toni began to climb the stairs carefully; worried in case someone should see her going where she was not supposed to be. Toni did what she often did when she was troubled. She pulled out her necklace and held her special owl in her hand. He would protect her; he would make sure she was safe.

Upstairs the rooms were totally deserted. Old broken desks and tables lay discarded, waiting to be repaired. There was an old blackboard lying sadly on its side, the last piece of work the children had been doing still written in neat chalk hand writing. Toni turned her head on the side trying to read it. It was one of those old boards that could be rotated round. The board was a sort of conveyor belt thing so the teacher could keep the board turning as they wrote.

Toni rubbed her hand on the chalky surface; her hand was white and dusty like she imagined the inside of all classrooms must have been. White boards were a much better idea she thought. In her classroom Mrs Johnson could project her computer screen onto the white board so the children could see it clearly. Chalk pictures in different colours must have taken ages to prepare, only to have them wiped away and forgotten.

It was just as well they had projectors now. Mrs Johnson's writing was dreadful; it was all scratchy and uneven. If she ever wrote anything by hand on her flip chart or white board, the children used to complain that they could not understand it. Once Mrs Johnson had had the cheek to say Toni's own writing was sometimes illegible!

There were piles of old school books on one of the tables. Toni thumbed through a few of them see what children had been learning. Her eyes opened wide as she realised she was looking at one of the first books she had ever read. The words were in huge black print with only one or two sentences to each page.

Toni could remember how she had struggled to get through the book, how she had stumbled over the words, how she had thought she would never ever get through to the end. Yet now she read through the whole book in a matter of seconds. When they had got their first dog, Toni had wanted to call him 'Floppy' too. It was strange how quickly things had changed. Toni had almost forgotten how to sound a word out now!

Chapter Three
Rose

There was a book on a table; it was an old, leather bound book. This could be the school's old log book, Mum had been telling her about. It certainly looked very important. As Toni picked it up something silver fell onto the table with a musical ring. She opened the book then flicked through the pages. It was hand written, every letter neatly joined to the next, in gently flowing script.

Toni wished she could write like that. Perhaps there was a font on her computer she could use. There was a date at the top of each page. The black writing seemed to fade, then become darker again after a few words. Toni stared at the writing closely. She understood how it had been written. The writer had used a pen which needed to be dipped into an ink well.

They had tried that out once in class. This was why, when the ink began to run out, the letters became faint. Sometimes the writer tried to make the ink last longer, then the end of a long word could hardly be read.

Toni closed the log book to read the title:

'Almund School'

Something was written inside the front cover in large letters.

'Turn the page to find out how we live."

Toni searched through the pages again until she came to the date she was interested in 17th September 1942. Toni began to read:

"Today a bomb landed on the school's air raid shelter....." "The story was there just as Toni had been told with the names of all the children too, exactly the same as the list she was soon going to read out loud.

Toni flicked through a few more pages; there was the lady her Mum had been talking about. It was easy to see, because the handwriting had changed its style.

"Today, I Agatha Booth have been appointed as head teacher of Almund School taking over after the sad loss of Miss Agnes Atkin ....

Toni put the book back where it had been. There was a silver disc on a chain lying on the table; it must have been lying on the book. Toni picked it up to look at it closely.

There was a flash of lightening through the window, which seemed for a moment to light up even the dustiest corners of the room.

"That's all we need today!" Toni said out loud. "Any moment now there will be a rumble of thunder and a downpour of rain."

Toni knew no matter how heavy the rain fell, Mr Cuthbert would still have them all sitting out on the playground. He wasn't someone to let a little weather spoil his plans.

She could hear him now, she knew what he would say: "The war didn't stop every time it rained you know! The soldiers had to carry on no matter what the weather was like!"

Toni imagined the whole school sitting in a torrential downpour, the rain soaked list crumbling in her hand as she attempted to read the blotched names. It was going to be a soggy disaster that only Mr Cuthbert would enjoy.

The time must be getting on a bit. Toni searched for her watch; then remembered that she didn't have it on today. Most children probably didn't have watches in those days, and they certainly did not wear them to come to school.

Mrs Johnson would be starting to wonder where Toni had got to; she had better head back to the classroom, though all the old stuff up here was far more interesting than the boring worksheets they had to do downstairs.

Toni began to pick her way down, making sure that she did not suddenly bump into Mr Cuthbert on her way. Suddenly a girl appeared on the stairs beside her. She must have been upstairs too because she was now hurrying past Toni on her way down. This is strange Toni thought:

I did not see anyone else up there. She must have been in one of the other classrooms I didn't go into.

Toni continued to slowly descend the stairs, keeping a continual wary eye open.

"Come on! You mustn't dawdle, we have got to hurry!"

The other girl grabbed Toni by the hand. Soon they were both running down the stairs as quickly as they could. Instead of turning towards her own classroom the girl made their way down a different flight of stone steps out into the play ground.

"I must have spent longer up there than I thought,"
Toni realised, "It must be time for the celebrations to begin. They must have sent the girl to look for me. Do I have time to look for an umbrella?"

Then Toni started to panic. She had left the list of names that she had to read out in her classroom. She had read them through so many times that she could probably have remembered them all off by heart. It would be a stupid thing to try to do. She had to go back for the list; they were all outside waiting for her.

Toni pulled away from the other girl.
"I have to go back, I left something in the classroom I have to go and get it."
Toni's arm was firmly grabbed and pulled in the direction of the playground.
"Don't be so stupid!" The girl was shouting now, "Didn't you hear the siren when it went off! You must be deaf or something. We were all told, when the siren goes off we have to stop what we are doing then hurry to the air raid shelter. There must be no going back for anything!"

Toni did not understand why the girl was being so silly, they were just re-enacting the day when all was said and done. Some people were taking things a too far.

"The air raid warden came into school on Tuesday. He told us that if we didn't move quickly we were putting not only our own lives in danger but the lives of those who would come to look for us too, so hurry up!"

Toni didn't remember any Air raid warden coming into school to talk to them. What was this stupid girl going on about?

She was now at the bottom of the stairs: It was where the girl's toilets should be. There was now nothing but row upon row of pegs on which coats could be hung: the toilets had somehow vanished into thin air!

Across the playground the two girls ran. A man in a tin hat was standing beside a large pile of sand bags. He was waving for them to hurry up.

"Sorry I am late Mr Warden, I found someone lingering in one of the rooms upstairs."

"That's alright Rose, you were right to bring her down here. It is OK. We have not heard the enemy planes going overhead yet. There is still time."

Toni eyed him blankly.

"You, young lady, should know better. When the air raid siren blows you have to move quickly! There must be no lingering about or dilly dallying, I shall be speaking to your mother about this you can rest assured!"

As the two girls were bundled down the steps into the shelter Toni could hear the distant drone of something slowly approaching overhead. Soon they were both seated at the end of a hard wooden bench. The shelter was crowded with children of all ages, some were crying, others chattering and some sitting very still, just listening to the noise outside.

A lady, she must have been a teacher, because when she spoke everyone stopped talking and listened to what she was saying. She suddenly began to sing:

> *"You are my sunshine,*
> *My only sunshine*
> *You make me happy*
> *When skies are grey*
> *You never know, dear,*
> *How much I love you"*

Then all of the children joined in with:

> *"Please don't take my sunshine away"*

The singing had the desired effect; soon there was no more crying and all the children were singing as loudly as they could. Even the distant 'crump, crump' that sounded like something exploding in the distance, was ignored.

Toni stared around the shelter, she knew no one in here. The teachers were all total strangers.
What was going on?
Who were all these people? Then a lady near her spoke to a child.

"Edna Cawthorn, yes you, will you please move up a little, poor Marjorie Turner is practically sitting on the floor!"

Edna Cawthorn, Marjorie Turner!

Toni had heard those names somewhere before. Suddenly she felt cold - her heart gave a loud resounding thump. Yes, she had heard those names before; they were on the list she was supposed to be reading out. Those were the names of two of the children who had been in the air raid shelter when the bomb dropped.

"Sorry Mrs Atkin," Edna mumbled, shuffling along the bench.

Agnes Atkin! Yet another name from the list. Toni searched for this Miss Atkin; she appeared to be the tall lady who was at least a head above all the others in the shelter. Then Toni noticed that Miss Atkin was wearing extraordinarily high heeled shoes, they seemed out of place here in an air raid shelter.

What am I doing? Toni realised, *I am sitting here inside an air raid shelter which is about to receive a direct hit from a bomb that will be dropped any second now!*

Toni stood up and shouted.

"Listen! All of you! You have to get out of here! You have to get out! Run as fast as you can!"

Heads turned in her direction and teachers scowled at her.

"You have to believe me! I know what is going to happen! We have to go now!"

Toni ran towards the entrance to the shelter, pushing a man who was standing there out of the way. Behind her she could hear screams and shouts as children began to panic, following her out of the door.

Soon a crowd, a throng, a mob of shrieking children were running as quickly as they could away from the shelter.

Wardens and teachers tried to stop them but the combined mass of tiny determined bodies was more than a match for the grown-ups. In seconds, everyone was out in the street, hurrying away behind the terrace of houses that faced the school.

The sky lit up with a burning light, a blast of fierce air rushed past them, flattening many to the ground.

Then the sound of the explosion erupted in Toni's ears, sending an excruciating pain surging to every corner of her being. Dust and rubble covered her. She was scratched and bruised. There was a deep cut above her eye, she could not move her legs, but at least she was alive.

Chapter Four
Bomb

Children lay stunned on the ground. A small wall had collapsed into a heap of bricks and mortar. A shattered chimney pot lay in the middle of the road. The bells of ambulances and fire engines filled the air as men and women in uniform descended upon the scene.

Slowly, one by one, the coughing children began to move. There were cut heads that needed attention, scraped knees and torn clothes. A few sat leaning against each other; their ears still ringing from the blast of the explosion.

Someone helped Toni to her feet after a large wooden beam pinning her legs had been carefully removed. In the school playground there was a scene of total destruction. The bomb had landed directly above the shelter. There was nothing left of it now, just a large, smoking, gaping hole in the ground.

Toni put her hand to her chest. Her lucky owl was missing. There wasn't even a leather chord around her neck. It had vanished completely. Rubble lay scattered everywhere. Bits of broken brick mingled with lumps of shattered plaster. The green owl had to be here somewhere. Toni wanted to stop and search for her owl, but she was led away by two men.

A whole side of the school had been blow away. Desks hung precariously; books and paper fluttered down in the breeze. In one room the teacher's desk had slipped, leaving it hanging by a single leg with the teacher's pink cardigan still wrapped round her chair.

An Air Raid Warden lay on a stretcher. He had a broken leg, but he would mend soon enough. A policeman was talking to him before the ambulance finally took him away.

"How many children do you think were in the shelter?" he asked nervously, expecting the worst.

"I don't understand it," The warden wondered, "a few seconds before the bomb landed, they all ran out. They escaped what would certainly have killed every single one of them!" He wiped the dust from his eyes.

"There was a girl, I don't know who she was, she shouted for them all to run! But for her, I dread to think what might have happened to them all. The bomb exploded right on top of the shelter. They would not have stood a chance."

"How many have been hurt?"

"I think I am the worst to be honest, though there is a little girl over there who I do not know: she just seems to be wandering around looking lost."

Parents had arrived from the houses around the school and once patched up, the walking wounded were taken home. There were a few that needed hospital attention but soon there were only the police, firemen and air raid wardens left to clear the scene.

Toni was on her own, standing by the remains of the shelter, wondering what she should do now.

"Come on little darling, there is nothing here for you. You had better get yourself off home." A policeman told her.

Toni was looking at the smoke, she didn't answer.

"What's the matter? Cat got your tongue? Come on there. What's your name, where do you live?"

"I am Toni Braithwaite; I live at 25 Heather Crescent." Toni replied.

"It's not near here is it? I don't know your street."

Toni shrugged her shoulders, "You go down the main road then turn left at the traffic lights. It's the second turning on the left."

"Traffic lights? There aren't any traffic lights in our town. I saw some in London when I was there before the war, but there aren't any here!"

"You don't have traffic lights? By the pub then, on the left," Toni was getting confused too now.

"Perhaps you have got the name a bit wrong, Heather Crescent? There is an Aster Crescent and a Heath Road?"

Toni shook her head; she didn't know what to say.

"Your voice is a bit different; you sound like you are not from round here. Are you an evacuee from Portsmouth or maybe even Southampton?"

Toni shook her head again, she knew what an evacuee was, and stated quietly:

"No, I have lived in this town all my life."

The policeman wasn't so sure; bomb explosions could have a strange effect on youngsters.

"Do you want me to walk you home?"

Toni nodded; she did not really know where she was. The streets were so very different. Some of the houses were the same but there weren't as many shops as she was used to.

The two walked hand in hand along the main road. There was hardly any traffic hurtling along, only a large green army lorry rumbled past. The men inside lifting the canvas cover to wave as they went by. Toni hardly had to wait a second to cross the road. The policeman was busy chattering about the exploding bomb.

"Someone told me a girl got them all to leave the shelter just before that bomb landed. Did you see her? Come to think of it, she probably saved everyone's life back there."

Toni peered down a side street. There were solid brick buildings all along the middle of the road. There was only just room for cars to get past. She wanted to ask what they were for, but when she saw a sign at the entrance to one of them saying 'Marlborough Road Shelter A': she managed to work it all out for herself.

Toni looked behind her, where the main road joined the street leading to her school there should have been busy roundabout. The road was narrow too; usually she had to stop in the middle of the road on a traffic island. It was impossible to walk straight across the busy road. Mum never ever let her do it on her own. There was nothing on the narrow road now.

Toni turned left where she thought the newspaper shop should be then continued along the road. She was soon out in the open countryside. There were farmer's fields on both sides of the road.

"Do you live in one of the farms?"

Toni shook her head. She knew she was looking at the street where her house was, but it was just a field, a field with cows grazing peacefully. There was a tall oak tree growing at the side of the road. It was different but she was sure it was the one standing in the pub garden.

"I think the big bang has shaken you up more than we thought it had." The policeman explained. "I will take you back to the station with me, I bet it won't be long before your mum comes looking for you. She must be at work. Is your dad in the army?"

Toni nodded, how would her mother ever find out where she was now? A tear began to drip down the side of her face.

Toni was well looked after at the police station. They put a warm blanket around her then she was given a cup of hot sweet tea made with condensed milk. Toni hated it but she was so tired and frightened, she drank it anyway.

The sergeant came and sat next to her. He wanted to find out a few more details.

"What is your name?" he asked.

"Toni," she replied.

"Tony! That's a boy's name! Is that what Mum calls you? Have you got another name?

"No I am Toni Braithwaite; I live at 25 Heather Crescent."

The sergeant looked over his shoulder at a policeman standing behind the desk nodding his head.

"We had better get Dr Ramsey to look at you."

Toni brightened up a little, she knew Dr Ramsey: she was really nice - pretty too! Toni had been to see her a few times, once when she had chicken pox, then again the time when she had stood on a nail and had to have an injection. Whatever was going on here at least she would know someone.

Chapter Five
Dr Ramsey

When Dr Ramsey finally arrived in the police station it was starting to get dark outside. Toni got a shock. Dr Ramsey was a man. He was just as nice though. Toni looked at him carefully. In many ways he looked just like the Dr Ramsey that she knew. There was something about his eyes that reminded her of the doctor she had seen before.

Dr Ramsey shone a light in Toni's eyes and took her temperature.
"I don't think there is anything to worry about," he smiled, "I think that loud bang has made you lose your memory for a while. Please do not worry! I am sure it will come back quickly."

Toni thanked the doctor, she was worried though. She had nowhere to go. Her home was not there anymore, she was lost in a different place and a very different time!
"Will I have to sleep in one of the police cells?" she asked. "I haven't done anything wrong."
A young policeman was just on his way home, he had a bag containing the remains of his lunch over his shoulder. PC Gregg had overheard what Toni was saying and had stopped to listen.

"Has this poor child got nowhere to go?" he asked.
The sergeant shook his head. It looked as though he was going to have to get in touch with the authorities in the morning to

see what could be done. That bomb seemed to have done something nasty to the girl's memory.

"Well, she is not staying in this draughty place all night. She can come home with me. My Lizzy will be glad of someone to play with."

Toni brightened up a bit, "How old is your Lizzy?" She asked.

"By the looks of you I would say she is about the same age as you are - and probably just as much trouble too. Come on, the missus said she was making a rice pudding for us tonight!"

The two left the police station walking the short distance to PC Gregg's house.

"My name is Tony, you can call me that; you don't want to be calling me Constable Gregg all night. What is yours?"

"I am called Toni too, Toni Braithwaite but my Toni is with an 'i' instead of a 'y'"

"Well Toni with an 'i' it is nice to meet you. I have never met a girl called Toni before. I have always thought that it was a boy's name!"

"Everyone keeps saying that," Toni continued, "My Mum says that it is short for Antonia. She said I was called Toni after someone who did something very important for our family. " At the thought of her mum, Toni went quiet for a few minutes.

"Which school do you go to Toni?"

"I thought that I went to Almund Primary School, but it all looks so different, I don't understand."

PC Gregg decided not to take the questioning any further. It was obvious the girl was tired and hungry. She would feel much better after a good night's sleep.

Mrs Gregg was surprised when her husband arrived home with a little visitor, but she didn't seem to mind much.

Lizzy was delighted there was someone new to play with. She took Toni by the hand and led her upstairs to her bedroom. Toni stared all round Lizzy's room. There was a bed in one corner, a small wardrobe in the other and old chest of drawers on which stood a few of Lizzy's things.

Toni thought that there was something important missing from the room but she couldn't work out what it was. She looked up at the ceiling and suddenly realised that there was no light.

"Where is the light?" Toni asked.

"We don't have any electricity upstairs yet," Lizzy told her, "Dad says that when the war is over we are going to have it all over the house!"

Toni was surprised; it was something she had never thought about, though she could remember her Grand pa saying something about having gas lights in the house once. He even showed her where the old gas lights used to stick out of the wall.

Lizzy was holding a moth eaten thing that might have once been covered in fur. "This is Taddy, he is my teddy bear."

"Can I hold him?" Toni asked.

Lizzy didn't look so sure, but she handed Taddy over.

Toni held the bear carefully. He had an eye missing, but a button had been sown in to replace it. Both paws had been patched several times.

"You must have had him a long time!" Toni thought.

"He used to be my Mum's teddy when she was little. Mum told me I was given a new one when I was small but I wouldn't let go of Taddy. We have been friends ever since. Do have you have a teddy bear?"

Toni felt glum, she had just realised that her own bear was still lying on her pillow at home. He had a small pink bow round his neck that had seen better days too.

"I don't know where he is." Toni sighed looking suddenly sad.

Lizzy understood - she would hate to lose Taddy.

There was a few minutes silence, Toni gave Taddy back to Lizzy then began to look at some of the books she had. There was a large book called 'The Pleasure Book for Boys and Girls.' Toni began to thumb through it.

"That's got a story by Enid Blyton in it!" Lizzy exclaimed. "Have you read any of her stories? I have got lots of them, they are great aren't they?"

Toni decided to change the subject.

"Do you have a television?" Toni asked, wondering if it was so late that she had missed all of her favourite programmes.

"Television? No, of course not! There hasn't been any television since before the war started. We didn't have one anyway. Dad is just a policeman."

"Oh!" Toni exclaimed, her voice sounding disappointed.

"Did you have a television in your house?" Lizzy asked.

"We had three, one in the front room, one in the kitchen and a portable one in my bedroom." Toni answered, not noticing the surprised expression on Lizzy's face.

"Three! I don't know anyone who has three televisions. I don't think even the king has that many!"

Toni didn't say anything.

Lizzy was calling downstairs."Mum! This girl is telling lies! She says she has three televisions on her house!"

Mum was going to pay no attention to her daughter's shout, but the sound of a furious argument soon brought her upstairs to see what was going on. They hadn't quite come to blows yet, but it was a close thing.

Dad was calling for his daughter to come down now.

"Your programme is just about to start," he reminded her.

Lizzy rushed for the door, closely followed by Toni.

"I thought you said you didn't have a television?" Toni called behind Lizzy.

"We don't, its Uncle Mac on the wireless!"

"Wireless? What's that?"

"Radio?" Lizzy answered.

Toni slowed down; she didn't see the point in rushing down just to listen to a radio! By the time Toni arrived in the front room Lizzy was sat on the floor next to her father and a 'tinny' voice from a large brown box in the corner was starting to tell a story about how the leopard got his spots.

That must be the radio Toni told herself. Her eyes followed a long wire that led to a large black thing on the floor. Toni had no idea what it was.

The room was dominated by a large upright piano that roughly filled the whole wall. There was a pair of brass candle sticks attached to the front of the piano on either side. The central music stand was stacked with music. 'The News Chronicle Song

Book' was open; Toni read the title of the piece that was still open, ready to be played. 'Flow gently Sweet Afton'. Toni had never heard of the song; it sounded dreadfully dull.

"Who is that reading the story?" Toni asked.

"It's Uncle Mac," Dad answered, "He tells a story every day on Children's hour. This week they are doing one of the 'Just So' stories, by Rudyard Kipling."

Toni had to admit it was nice. It must have been good for Lizzy to cuddle up to her Dad for a story. It never happened in her house.

It was a good story too; she liked the description of the jungle. It said it was:

" Speckled and sprottled, and spottled, dotted and splashed and slashed and hatched and cross-hatched with shadows. "

It was quite a tongue twister to try to say.

Once the story was over, Mum called for them to come into the kitchen, where she had laid the table for tea. There was a cloth on the table. They even had side plates and cups with saucers too. It was just like having dinner at her Aunty Maureen's.

There was buttered bread on a plate in the middle of the table, a pot of jam in a silver container. There was an absolutely delicious cake too that cried out to be eaten.

Mum could see that Toni had her eyes on the cake.

"I hope you like carrot cake Toni; I made it from a recipe I saw in the paper."

"You made it?" Toni's voice sounded surprised. "My mum never does any baking; she gets all her cakes from the supermarket. I wish she did though! It looks scrummy!"

Mum laughed, "You are a one Toni, we don't have any 'super' markets here just the ordinary ones."

"Someone at school says they got things from the black market, is that the same?" Lizzy asked.

"No Lizzy it certainly is not! There is a war on; people who sell things on the black market are not helping our country to win the war. They are helping that horrid Mr Hitler!"

At the mention of his name Mum and Lizzy both shouted, "Boo!" so Toni joined in too.

There was a large pot of tea under a woollen thing; Toni thought must be a tea cosy. She had seen a picture of one in a book, but had never actually seen one being used before.

"Have you been to America?" Lizzy asked Toni.

Toni explained she had never been there.

"When you mentioned all those televisions, then 'super' markets, I thought it must be somewhere you have been."

"Toni was very near to a bomb when it exploded," Dad explained, "She has lost some of her memory, maybe she has been to America but can't think about it just now." He put a friendly hand on Toni's shoulder. "Don't worry Toni, memories are funny things, yours will be back soon." Toni smiled. She liked Lizzy's dad - he was kind and understanding just like any policeman should be.

*Chapter Six
Red Rover

When they had all finished tea, Toni felt quite full. She had eaten lots of bread and jam with a huge slice of carrot cake, which turned out to be just as good as it seemed.

Toni had never really liked rice pudding but there was something about Mrs Gregg recipe made it irresistible.

"Can we go out to play for a little while?" Lizzy asked.

Toni was quite shocked; her Mum never let her play out in the street. There were far too many cars going past. There were strangers too, it would be too dangerous. She was only ever allowed go to play in the park if someone went with her.

Lizzy's Mum pulled aside the thick curtains from the window; it was still quite light out there.

"Alright Lizzy, you can take Toni with you, but if you here the siren you must hurry straight home as quickly as you can."

"It's OK, Mum; we will only be outside in the street. I can see some of the others there."

Soon both girls were outside. Lizzy's friends were playing 'Red Rover' so they joined in. The children were a real motley crew. Most of the girls were wearing dresses of various colours. Some had little white collars, other had tight belts. There wasn't a pair of sparkly jeans to be seen. All of their dresses all looked as though they had been washed many times as the colours were faded and dull.

The boys were all wearing short trousers held up with braces over their baggy shirts. There was a pile of jumpers at the side of the road which had been their goal posts before the game had started.

Two boys were running round with their arms out further down the street. They were shouting to each other and making strange noises.

"Red leader you are clear for take off!"

"Roger Wilco!"

They are playing at being spitfires, Toni realised.

Toni couldn't help noticing the girls' hair: it was dull and lifeless. Had they never heard of extra protein balanced conditioner?

This year's fashion seemed to be pink cardigans, but it would be a huge mistake to have the buttons done up.

Toni thought it was strange; some of the girls were a lot older than any she had played with before. She was used to seeing teenagers fussing around with their phones and iPods; perhaps makeup and boyfriends hadn't been invented yet either.

Toni had never played 'Red Rover' before, so she tried to watch and see if she could pick it up quickly.

Two older girls stood in the middle of the road with their hands joined, everyone else lined up against the wall.

"Red Rover, Red Rover, call Peter right over!"

Peter, who was a little younger than Lizzy and Toni, had to try to run across the road. He wasn't good at it and he was soon caught between the other two girls. They obviously knew he was slow to run, so he had to join hands with them to get ready to catch the next person.

"Red Rover, Red Rover, call **Toni** right over!"

"What do I have to do?" Toni asked, beginning to panic a bit.

"You have to run into their hands and try to break through the chain they make."

Toni ran as fast as she could, aiming for where Peter held onto one of the older girls. She soon burst right through and got to the other side.

"Whoa Mamma!" Toni shouted jumping up and down.

For a second everyone stared at her, wondering what on earth she was saying, then there was a mad scramble, as the all children tried to run across the road. Two of the younger kids were caught in the hubbub. They were reluctantly joined onto the chain.

The 'spitfire boys' approached, dodging in and out of children as they ran across the road, attempting to shoot them down. They were soon chased away by some other boys who became German Messerschmitts.

Toni thought 'Red Rover' was a good game to play outside. She was amazed there were no cars honking at them to get out of the way. They had the entire street to themselves. Mum would have gone completely berserk if she had played in the street at home. Gradually the light began to dim. There was a street lamp on the corner, but it did not come on. Toni wondered about the windows of the houses. She was expecting to see them lit up as people turned on their lights inside their homes, but all the windows stayed dark, with no light escaping from inside.

Lizzy could see her Mum standing on the doorstep ready to call her in, so she and Toni shouted good night to all of their friends then hurried inside. Inside Lizzy's dad was hammering away at the piano trying to sing along to the music. Lizzy pulled Toni away, sometimes it was better not to be in the same room as her father when he was singing.

Up in Lizzy's bedroom Mum had been making the bed. Toni had been wondering where she was going to sleep; now she knew. There was a pillow at each end of the bed so they could sleep 'top to tail,' as Lizzy's Mum called it.

Toni found it difficult to get to sleep. Lizzy had started to snore. Every time she turned over, she accidentally kicked Toni. Toni was missing her Mum and Dad. She didn't know what had happened to them. She didn't know if they would be looking for her. They must be worried too, Toni thought. She wished she could tell them that she was alright, but there was no way she could get any messages back to them. She was also missing the company of her Teddy, so she tied the corner of the sheet into a thick knot and cuddled up to it instead.

Toni was trying hard to be brave, but she found the complete darkness of her bedroom disturbing. She was used to having the light from a lamppost outside her room. At home there would be the noise of cars passing by throughout the night, their headlamps splashing a beam of light over her bedroom walls as they went by. In this room, it was total darkness.

PC Gregg had stopped singing, so the only sound was the distant rumble of the radio downstairs with the occasional burst of laughter as Lizzy's Mum and Dad laughed out loud at something they had heard.

Toni must have eventually dropped off to sleep because she was suddenly woken by a torch being shone in her eyes.
"Quick! Both of you! You have to get up!"
For a moment or two Toni thought she was back in her own bedroom, but Lizzy's grumbling voice quickly brought her back to reality. Lizzy was out of bed wearing a thick woollen dressing gown. Mrs Gregg was holding a coat open so she could wrap it round Toni's shoulders.
"What's the matter?" She blearily asked.
"Air raid! Come on, we have get to the shelter!"

Toni and Lizzy staggered out, almost falling down the stairs as they were led towards the back door. In the back garden three families had already assembled in the underground air raid shelter that had been built across the back gardens. In the distance they could hear the whirling noise of the siren as it signalled its warning.

Inside the shelter, children were already tucked up in bunk beds. Lizzy was lifted into her place looking as if she was hardly awake; she was obviously used to being woken up in the middle of the night. A place was soon found for Toni. The bed was hard and uncomfortable. Her head was near the ceiling and she imagined hoards of spiders were already climbing up the shelter walls to invade her peace.

The room shook violently as an explosion rocked the whole bed. Toni was sure it had been lifted clean off the floor.

"That was close!"

"Too close if you ask me mate!"

There was a tap on the door and a blast of cold air blew in as a figure entered.

"Brunswick Street has got it!" A man announced. "A fire engine is on its way but we need you Constable Gregg. Lizzy's dad could be heard mumbling something about his boots, and then he was gone.

Another huge explosion came. This one was even nearer, soil from the garden above trickled down into Toni's eyes. She curled up tight in the blanket, keeping her eyes tight shut. Maybe, if she hid, it would all go away.

The sudden vibrations the bombs made felt like earthquakes. The door was constantly opening, allowing the cold night air laced with dense smoke to pervade the room. Hushed voices could be heard, coupled with sighs. Sometimes there were angry exclamations. Toni knew something bad had happened: she was worried and she could not sleep.

As she lay in her solid bunk bed she tried to work out how it had happened. She had left the classroom after asking to be excused, then, instead of going to the girl's toilets; she had decided to go for a wander around her school. She had climbed up the stairs to a part of the school which was no longer used. She had seen piles of old books. She had even rummaged through some of them. She could remember the broken furniture and the abandoned black board lying pathetically on its side.

Something must have happened, because the next thing she knew she was being led down the stairs again by a girl. Toni searched her memory for the one thing that might have caused the change. There was an old book on a table. It was a really old dusty book. Mum had been telling her about the school log book. This must have been it. Toni remembered picking it up and reading it, but no matter how hard she tried she couldn't recall what she had read on the first page.

Chapter Seven
Trevor

When Toni woke up it was a new day. There was light streaming through the bedroom window. A kick from Lizzy told her she was back inside the house again. How she had got there, she did not know.

Lizzy's Mum was standing by the door smiling.
"We carried you back to bed last night; you were so fast asleep no one could wake you up!"
Toni stretched her arms wondering what sort of day lay ahead for her.
"Hurry up, breakfast is ready!"
Lizzy crawled out of bed looking as bleary eyed as Toni felt. She was still not used to having to get up in the middle of the night.

The two girls were soon dressed and hurrying down to the kitchen. There was a boy sitting at the table. He was wearing short trousers held up with black braces that went over his faded blue shirt. His brown jacket was on the back of his chair. He still had his school cap on his head.

"What is Trevor doing here?" Lizzy asked recognising one of the boys from her class.
"He lives in Brunswick Street," Mum began to explain, "They had a bomb there last night."

Lizzy was surprised, "Are you all right Trevor?" she asked.

Trevor did not reply he was staring at the table, a small silver aeroplane held tightly in his hand.

"What's that you have got?" Toni asked stretching out a hand to look at Trevor's plane.

"It's mine! Leave it alone!" Trevor pushed the plane deep into his pocket then turned away from Lizzy and Toni.

"Trevor and his Mum didn't go to the shelter last night," Mum was telling them, "They mustn't have heard the warning siren when it went off so they were both in the house when a bomb dropped."

Toni was shocked, "Are Trevor's parents safe?" she asked.

"Trevor's Mum has been taken to hospital, she is going to be better soon, but she has a broken leg, so Trevor is going to stay here until we can get in touch with his Aunt."

"What about his Dad?" Toni continued.

Mum's voice became hushed. "Mr Barat is a pilot in the Royal Air Force. His plane was shot down over France a few weeks ago. There hasn't been any news yet. He may have been captured or he might be trying to get back, we don't know yet."

Trevor lifted his head up from the table, "My Dad is on his way home. He will be hiding in farm yards during the day then travelling throughout the night. As soon as he gets to Spain, he will send me a message!"

Lizzy pulled Toni to one side, "He has been reading one of those dreadful comics, they are full of stories about escaping pilots! He thinks his Dad is one of them."

"He may be right!" Toni confirmed. Lizzy's face told her she did not believe a word of it.

"Over five hundred pilots have been killed." Lizzy whispered.

"As soon as you have all had some breakfast, Trevor can walk to school with you." Mum was telling them. She was carrying a large steaming pan of porridge and poured some out for each of them. Toni searched round the table for the sugar, but she was not very surprised when she couldn't find any.

Soon the children were on their way to school. They each carried a small cardboard box on a string round their necks. When Toni was given a spare one, she thought it had something to eat in it, but there was just a funny looking rubber object inside.

"Don't forget to take your gas masks will you!" Mum reminded them all.

Trevor had brightened up a lot now he had had some breakfast. He was ready to tell the girls what had happened.

"I was lying in bed last night, with the blankets pulled up round my head. Then I think I must have been woken up by the bomb. There was soil and dust falling down around my eyes - I had to rub them to get it out! When I opened my eyes, I could see the stars up above and I saw a search light streaming over the sky. It took a minute before I realised the roof of our house had gone!"

"You mean you could actually see the sky?"

Trevor nodded.

"I hurried downstairs to see what was happening. I heard my Mum shouting for someone to help her, but I could not get into her bedroom; something was blocking the door."

"Your house must have been very badly damaged. You were so lucky not to be killed!"

"Then these men came in. They were all wearing helmets. I thought the Germans had landed and we were being invaded. I grabbed a bit of wood from the staircase and started hitting them with it. I smacked one of them right on his mouth!"

Lizzy and Toni stared with their mouths wide open.

"But it wasn't the Germans after all; it was the air raid wardens coming in to help rescue me and my Mum!"

Toni was laughing. "Did you really hit him in the mouth?"

Trevor was laughing too,

"He had a big cut on his lip; I think he had to go to hospital as well as Mum. They took her away on a stretcher."

"I hope your Mum will be better soon." Lizzy told him.

"She made me promise to go to school and try my best. She wants Dad to be proud of me when he gets home."

Toni desperately wanted to get back into school. She wanted to look in the rubble for her owl. She also thought if she went back up stairs, she might find the log book again. She was sure there was something important on the book's first page, if only she could remember what it was.

Firemen and Wardens could be seen picking through the rubble which had once been part of the school. A large wagon was quickly being filled. Once they had made the building safe, the gates would be firmly locked, barring anyone from going inside.

By now the children were standing outside their school, waiting with the other children for the gates to be opened. They were late this morning. Then the head teacher came out and held her hands up for all to be quiet so she might talk to them.

A truck loaded with rubble stopped her from talking as it rumbled past. Toni saw the playground was already cleared. Her owl was now somewhere among all the bricks in the back of the lorry.

"I am sorry boys and girls but our school has been badly damaged. As you all know, a bomb landed on the air raid shelter yesterday. The explosion not only destroyed the shelter but it also caused the collapse of part of the wall. We hope get it all repaired soon, but as we know only too well there is a war on and it will take some time, so until further notice the school will remain closed."

There was a loud cheer from the children as they realised they would no longer have to go to school. From now on, every day was going to be one continual holiday.

Toni was devastated. She was starting to panic! If she didn't do something soon, she would be stuck in war torn England until the war was over.

Toni had one comforting thought. At least she knew the war would be over in 1945. Germany would be defeated. The bombing and fighting would stop one day but her new friends knew nothing about the future.

Toni and Lizzy began to walk home to tell Lizzy's Mum the school was not going to be open for a while. Trevor had met up with some of his friends. They all decided they were going to go exploring on some of the nearby bomb sites to see if they could find any pieces of bomb lying around. Bits of shrapnel were the real trophies they all wanted to collect. Trevor said when he had enough bits he was going to stick them all back together again and make a bomb of his own. He had it all worked out. If Hitler came, he was going to be ready for him.

Chapter Eight
The Library

Mum was not happy. "What are you going to do with yourselves all day if there is no school?" She asked.

Lizzy was happy, she thought it was going to be wonderful to be able to go out to play all day every day.

Mum was busy doing the washing and ironing. She did not really want to have the children under her feet all the time.

"Why don't we go to the library?" Toni suggested.

"The library? That's just as bad as going to school!" Lizzy was not impressed.

"We can't just wander around all day with nothing to do! It will be even more boring."

Lizzy reluctantly agreed to go to the library with Toni, even though she would far rather have gone to the bomb sites with Trevor.

The library was one of the few buildings in the centre of town not to have been damaged by air raids, though there were bags of sand piled up high against the walls making the entrance difficult to find. Toni and Lizzy climbed up three wide steps into a small hallway. On each side there were colourful posters pinned up.

Toni had not seen any of these before. In her library there were only notices about books or special events the librarian was holding.

One caught her eye: 'Always carry your gas mask! Hitler will send no warning!'

"Why do we need gas masks?" Toni asked.

Lizzy was astounded that she did not know. "The Germans are going to drop gas bombs on us. If you breathe in the gas you will be killed. I thought everyone knew that!"

"Oh yeah! I forgot!" Toni didn't sound convincing.

There was a poster that made her really start to laugh out loud. It was a picture of an older man in some kind of army uniform, the poster announced:

'Men aged 41-55. Let them all come!'

Toni wanted to say, 'They're Dad's Army.' She recognised the uniform. She half expected to see Captain Mainwaring with Corporal Jones walking down the street towards her.

"What are you smiling about?" Lizzy asked.

"Don't panic! Don't panic!" Toni laughed, grabbing her friend by the arm.

"What 'panic'?" Lizzy was confused.

They pulled a highly polished brass handle and then walked through the glass panelled door into the library. She had been in here so many times. The doors were exactly the same as she remembered, but here the glass doors had criss-crosses of brown paper covering them. Some of the panes seemed to be a cracked and damaged thanks to the bombs. Toni knew they would all look as good as new one day.

There was a friendly old lady standing behind the desk in the library. Toni went to ask her where the books for children were kept. A frail finger pointed towards a small shelf at the far end of the room.

Toni ran her eyes along the shelf for something which might attract her attention. There were no 'Harry Potters, Roald Dahls or Jacqueline Wilson' books for her to read, though there was a complete set of Beatrix Potter books which she liked and some books by A. A. Milne, including a 'Winnie the Pooh.' Lizzy picked up a well thumbed book by Enid Blyton, Toni told her to put it back. There had to be something better on the shelves.

One lady was putting books back on the shelves. "No school for you today girls?" She asked.

"Sadly no," Toni answered, "Our school was bombed yesterday so it has been closed because it is too dangerous." She was going to add, 'For health and safety reasons' but that kind of comment was a few years away.

"Sadly! I would have thought you would be happy to be missing school!"

The frail lady behind the counter made a hush sound and put one finger to her lips, the other hand was pointing to a sign that said 'SILENCE'.

Toni giggled to herself then explained in a hushed voice, "No, I love going to school! I love reading and writing. I know I am going to get bored and fed up just wandering round the streets all day."

Lizzy was shaking her head in strong disagreement.

"Well you can come in here any time you like. We have got all of the 'Encyclopaedia Britannica' on a shelf over there, so if there is anything you need to know, just look it up!"

Toni wished they were connected to the Internet too, but it was going to take a long time for that to happen.

There was a small book which seemed to poke out from the shelf towards Toni's hand: Old Possum's Book of Practical Cats. She had never read the book, but her Mum had taken her to see the musical 'Cats' when they were in London a while ago. She loved the music and the dancing but had never got round to reading any of the poems themselves.

Toni took the book of poems down from the shelf and started to read it.
"What have you got there?" Lizzy asked
"It's a poetry book," Toni told her.
"Oh yuck! Poetry. That is so boring - I bet it is dreadful."
"No it's not, it's good, listen."
In her best, most dramatic, voice, Toni began to read 'Macavity'. Toni had heard the music many times so as she read the poem out loud she could hear the rhythm of the singing in the background even though it wasn't there.

"Macavity's a Mystery Cat: he's called the Hidden Paw—
For he's the master criminal who can defy the Law.
He's the bafflement of Scotland Yard, the Flying Squad's despair:
For when they reach the scene of crime—Macavity's not there!"

The library was already quiet, but as Toni recited the poem, it became even more still. People who were busy looking for a book stopped what they were doing and listened to every word Toni was saying. Even the frail old lady behind the counter leaned forward so her large hearing aid could pick up the sound.

Macavity, Macavity, there's no one like Macavity,
There never was a Cat of such deceitfulness and suavity.
He always has an alibi, and one or two to spare:
At whatever time the deed took place
—MACAVITY WASN'T THERE!

And they say that all the Cats whose wicked deeds are widely known
(I might mention Mungojerrie, I might mention Griddlebone)
Are nothing more than agents for the Cat who all the time
Just controls their operations: the Napoleon of Crime!

By the time Toni got to the end of the poem, only a dropped pin from a grenade, would have disturbed the atmosphere she had created. Lizzy had a huge smile on her face and had raced over so she could see the words as Toni read them.

Toni stopped reading, a resounding burst of applause echoed round the whole of the library. An older man came over to pat Toni on the head and press a silver sixpence into her hand. Toni could not believe what had happened! It was something she would never have dared to do at home.

Toni noticed the clock on the wall. It was time they both hurried back to Lizzy's Mum, she would be wondering where they were. A lady came out of the back office. She

She had her hair tied back in a tight bun and was dressed in a coarse tweed skirt and jacket. She looked as old as any of the dusty books on the shelves. A tiny pair of half glasses balanced on her nose. She was obviously in charge.

She came towards Toni and Lizzy, her dark brown brogues clumping on the wooden floor as she approached. The girls felt apprehensive as she drew near. Were they going to get told off for making a noise? Would she throw them out and ban them for creating a disturbance?

"My dear girl! That was a truly wonderful rendition of a marvellous poem. I am sure our ladies' 'afternoon tea' club would love to hear you recite some more of those poems. Can I book you in to come here on Tuesday at 3 o'clock?"

Toni was astounded and could only mumble a, "Yes, of course," as she and Lizzy hurried towards the door, eager to be on their way home.

Chapter Nine
Batemans

Lizzy burst through her front door, shouting to her Mum.

"Mum! We went to the library and you will never guess what happened...!"

She stopped dead in her tracks. There was a lady she did not know sitting in the front room. She had a cup of tea balanced on the arm of her chair and a slice of cake on a plate. Lizzy stared at the lady: Her leg was in plaster, propped up on a little stool. In spite of her makeup, the girls noticed the lady had a large bruise over her eye. Her head had a cut that had been stitched closed: it must have been painful. It didn't take them long to work out whom the lady was; it had to be Trevor's mother, home from the hospital.

"You must be the girl with the unusual name," Mrs. Vickers said staring at Toni. I have been hearing all about you from Anne here."

Mrs. Gregg came in from the kitchen wiping her hands on a towel.

"I thought Trevor was with you two. Where did he go?"

Lizzy was standing next to Toni; she gave Toni a knowing nudge.

"I think he went over to the park to play football with some of his friends."

"I don't like him hanging round with that lot," Mrs. Vickers explained, "They are always smoking and they keep going off to play on the bomb sites. I read in the paper the other day a young boy lost his hand when he started to play with one of those 'century' things the Germans drop on us."

Toni met Lizzy's eyes. They were both wondering what Mrs. Vickers was trying to tell them.

"Oh! That sounds terrible. Some of those *incendiary* bombs don't go off when they are dropped; they just lie around waiting for someone to pick them up!" Mrs Gregg agreed, looking meaningfully at the girls.

"It's so typical of Hitler; it will be our turn to drop stuff on him soon." Mrs Vickers growled angrily up at the sky and shook her fist."Just you wait when our planes start flying over Germany. You will be sorry!"

Just then Trevor came in; he was carrying something behind his back.

"Mum!" He shouted, "You are home - I mean you're back!"

He went over to give his Mum a hug, making sure he did not bang into her leg but managing to not turn his back towards anyone else in the room.

"Are we going to stay here with Mrs. Gregg until the house gets fixed up?"Trevor asked.

Mum had some news to tell her son.

"No, we are going to stay with my sister, Alice."

"Oh no! Please not Aunty Ali! Can't we stay here?"

Mum would have put her foot down, if it had not been encased in plaster.

"Aunty Alice is good. She has a big house out in the countryside. You will have a room all to yourself and we won't have to go hiding in a shelter every night!"

"But Mum, she is so strict. She makes me clean my teeth. I had to have a bath last time we went to stay."

"Trevor dear, it was your own fault; you shouldn't have tried to climb over the farm wall!"

Lizzy and Toni waited, there had to be more to this story.

"He jumped off the wall and landed right in the middle of a big pit full of horse's you know what!"

Toni and Lizzy were quickly helpless with laughter.

"No one told me it was there!" Trevor complained.

"Where have you been anyway Trevor? And what is that you are hiding behind your back?"

"Nothing! We were helping Mr. Bateman in the shop. He needed some boxes stacking up at the back."

"Did you see him get any deliveries while you were there?" Lizzy's Mum questioned.

"I think he has, there was a queue stretching out onto the pavement when I left."

Mrs. Gregg and Mrs. Vickers were both alarmed and excited at the news.

"A queue? He must have something that is off the ration! I had better get down there and see what he has got." Lizzy's Mum had her coat on and was out of the door before she had finished speaking.

Toni stood still, watching and wondering what all the fuss was about.

"Last week Mr. Bateman had some packets of rice." Lizzy explained, "We haven't been able to get any for months. Mum was just passing the shop when it came in so she was able to get some. We had rice pudding for a week!"

PC Gregg had met his wife as she was leaving the house. He had a man with him.

"Toni, this is Mr. Albert, he is from the Tuther Chronicle. He wants to talk to you about the bomb that landed on the school shelter."

Toni felt unsure and very uncomfortable. She was uncertain about what to admit to and what people would say if she told all of her story.

"He would like to take your picture and put something in the paper about you. You are something of a hero around here. It was thanks to you a lot of children were not killed!"

Mr. Albert had a large red face. He must have been facing the wrong way when a fire bomb dropped. His hair was stuck up in the air like the brush it surely needed. He asked Toni to come and sit down while he made some notes in his book.

Toni didn't know what to say. If she told him the truth he would think the exploding bomb had made her quite mad and stupid. Worse than that, he might think she was a liar and get her into an even more awkward situation!

She decided to tell him she didn't really remember much about it. She could only just recall going into the shelter, what with the bomb and everything, her mind was quite blank.

"I think if we put your picture in the paper, then maybe someone will recognise you and come forward and help us all to find out where your family is." He said kindly.

Lizzy was impressed. She had never had her picture in the paper. No one had ever written anything about her. Toni could see Lizzy was excited.

"Can Lizzy be in the picture with me? You could say we have become good friends because of the bomb and Lizzy's Mum and Dad are looking after me too."

Mr. Albert thought this was a good idea.

"It will show how the people of our town are helping each other during this terrible war."

He made a few notes and then produced an enormous camera from his bag. He got Lizzy and Toni to stand together by the front door so he framed the picture better. Trevor wanted to be in the picture too, but Mr. Albert thought it would make it look too crowded.

"You will probably end up with the whole street in the picture if the children round here have their way." Mrs Vickers stated.

Mr. Albert thought having a picture of all the children would be good for another story he was writing for the paper. It was going to be about the school being closed because of the bomb damage, but that was for a later day, when the light was much better.

Trevor raced off to tell all of his friends they were going to have their picture in the paper.

Lizzy's Mum came bustling into the house, she was all smiles and happy.

"You look like you had a successful trip to the shops," said Mrs Vickers smiling.

"I have! Mr Bateman is a lovely man; he had heard how we have two children staying with us until they can be with their own family, so you will never guess what he had for me!"

Mrs Vickers waited with bated breath.

"Only four large lamb's hearts! Isn't that amazing?"

Toni felt something beginning to gag in her throat.

Lambs hearts?' Were they really going to have to eat them?

"And that's not all!" Lizzy's Mum grinned as though she had just won the lottery,

"He had just had a delivery of marmalade. He let me have a large jar even though I don't have a ration card for Toni! I promised I would give him the coupons as soon as her card came through!"

Chapter Ten
Tuther Chronicle

It was quite a night in the Gregg household. Trevor was to have the bed in the box room. Lizzy and Toni would be sleeping top to tail again. PC Gregg was on night duty so the two ladies decided to share the double bed since he was away.

PC Gregg would be busy all night, keeping the town safe. If there was an air raid he would be making sure no criminals took advantage of the empty houses and shops to go about their criminal behaviour. He had already caught two well known villains a few nights ago. They had climbed out of a broken shop window and practically fallen over him.

In the winter he had caught one would be burglar by following his footsteps back to his home. The poor man did not understand how the police had managed to catch up with him so quickly. He can't have noticed that it was snowing at the time!

However, things were not to work out how everyone had hoped. The moment Toni had managed to swallow her last fork full of braised heart, the siren started to call out its warning, so they all decamped quickly to the air raid shelter.

"We can leave the washing up for Mr Hitler to do!" Mum ventured to say, as she closed the door and headed towards safety.

It was a bit too early for the children to all snuggle down in bed, so they all huddled round a radio an enterprising neighbour had managed to rig up for them.

"There is no way Goering is going to make me miss 'IT-MA' again!" he explained.

"I just hope no one trips over the wire and knocks my accumulator over, we don't want acid everywhere as well as bombs!"

Toni saw a funny black thing like the one Lizzy's parents had connected to the radio; she still had no idea what it was.

The girls were sitting on their bunk bed, their legs dangling over the edge, a thick blanket wrapped round them both.

"What's 'IT-MA'?" Toni asked Lizzy.

"You don't know? I thought everyone did! It's Mr Tommy Handley's radio show, it's short for 'It's That Man Again.' I like Mrs Mopp best, she always says, 'Can I do you now sir?'" Lizzy was trying to do the character's voice. She wasn't very good but there was laughter when a neighbour chimed in with,

"I don't mind if I do! "

The air raid warden came in to see if there was any tea brewed but he was hardly able to move inside the crowded shelter. Word had got round that IT-MA would be on in there.

"Excuse me, can I get past please?" The warden asked.

"After you Cedric!" a man said closing the door. "No, after you Cecil," came the reply. They were laughing so much they hardly noticed the programme had started.

Toni did not understand any of the banter that went on between the characters but she couldn't help laughing along with them all. Their enjoyment of the programme was quite infectious. It made them all able to forget about the rumble of the bombing going on outside.

In the sky wave after wave of enemy planes came over all heading for their special targets. Tonight Tuther escaped any further damage, but everyone knew, not far away, families would be waking up in the morning to discover their homes had been flattened and their most precious possessions blasted to the four winds. Nothing was safe.

When morning finally arrived, all of the families were still inside the shelter. The raid had continued for most of the night with the final wave only departing just as the sun was beginning to lighten the sky.

PC Gregg had the kettle boiled and ready for a hot cup of tea as they all dragged themselves back to the kitchen. He had one of those large black accumulator things on the floor.

"Oh I see you managed to get it charged up! I was worried that it would run down and leave us with no power for the radio!" Mum said.

"Bentley's never let us down, one day soon we won't have to go humping a heavy accumulator around just so we can listen to the radio!"

He also had something for Toni that he had picked up at the newsagents on his way home.

Toni could not believe the front page of the 'Tuther Chronicle' a picture of herself next to Lizzy was given pride of place, along with the headline:

Mystery Girl is Local Hero

Almund School escaped what could have been a devastating disaster when Toni Braithwaite, pictured above with Elizabeth Gregg, shouted for everyone to get out of the shelter as quickly as they were able. Toni who has been badly affected by the bombs blast cannot remember anything that happened in the shelter.

But for Toni, many children and teachers would surely have met their end. The enemy bomb fell directly onto the school's air raid shelter, destroying it totally. A few children received nothing more than cuts and scratches. Toni herself seems to have fared worse than anyone.

She does not even know who her family are and where she comes from. The Chronicle asks all in Tuther to look at her picture and let us know if you recognise her or remember her name. She is currently living with a member of our Police Force where she is being excellently cared for.

Toni was not sure she liked the picture in the paper. Lizzy had a huge smile, but Toni's face seemed as though someone was poking her in the back with a pin! The paper was passed around the table with PC Gregg reading the piece about Toni out loud so they all might hear it. He strongly expected some of the words might be a too hard for Trevor to cope with,

"We will have to wait and see if anyone recognises Toni or can tell us anything about her. The doctor was hoping Toni would start to remember things soon, but it may be that the bomb may have wiped part of her memory for good."

Toni had to pretend to be alarmed. She knew she did not have anything wrong with her; it was just that she was unable to tell anyone the truth about who she was or where she actually came from.

Mum was busy getting breakfast ready for everyone. After a night in the shelter, she thought they all needed more than a bowl of porridge, so she had decided to use up the whole family's weekly ration of bacon and eggs to make everyone a proper breakfast!

Chapter Eleven
Grand Pa

For once, PC Gregg did something he rarely contemplated. He used his position as a police constable to pull a few strings and get Toni a ration card. This would not only make it easier for his wife to get food for the family; it also helped her find something for Toni to wear.

Apart from the clothes she was standing up in, Toni had had to borrow things from Lizzy. Both girls were growing quickly so there was little that would actually fit them both. Mrs Gregg was proficient with needle and thread but there was only so much 'making do and mending' that she could do. Hems and seams had already been let out twice, any more and Lizzy's clothes were in danger of falling off her!

Mrs Gregg took both girls to a second hand shop to see if there was anything there that would do for either of them. Toni searched all along the rails of clothes to see if she could find a pair of jeans and a t shirt, but there was nothing like that. She was going to have to wear a dress. A dress! She would normally have rather been shot at dawn than wear a dress.

When Toni's Aunty had got married, Toni had been a bridesmaid. There was a long purple satin dress for her to wear. Mum told her she was gorgeous, Dad beamed he was so proud of her. Toni wanted to have a brown paper bag over her head in case anyone she knew from school actually saw her wearing it.

When the photographer came to the reception to take some pictures, Toni hid in the toilets and was only coaxed out with promises of chocolate.

They left the shop with three dresses, all of them far too big for either of the girls, but Mrs Gregg thought it would not take her long to sort the problem out.

Mrs Gregg used the clothing coupons on Toni's ration book to buy her plenty of socks and underwear, Toni was glad - she had a thing about sharing someone else's knickers.

Mrs Gregg also managed to find an 'almost new' jumper.

"It is far too big for either of us." The girls complained. Mrs Gregg told them she was going to unravel all the wool, and then knit it up again. She would probably have enough wool for hats, scarves and gloves for both of them.

Toni sat watching Lizzy's Mum as she started to knit. The needles seemed to fly as they clicked the stitches into place. Mum noticed Toni's interest.

"Would you like to have a try at knitting, Toni?" she said.

"I had a try with my Nan a while ago, but I got into a real muddle."

Mum found some large needles and an old odd end of wool she had in her knitting bag. She cast on a few stitches for Toni and then carefully showed her how to start:

"In, over, through and off"

'All that to make a single stitch' she thought but it wasn't long before Toni had completed a whole row of knitting. Lizzie's Mum watched and corrected and encouraged her, so soon she was managing to knit without even looking at what she was doing.

Lizzy came into the room, she wanted to have a go at knitting too. Soon both girls were in competition with each other, racing to see who could do a row first. Mum was quite amazed because even though they were racing along, they did not make many mistakes.

Lizzy decided she was going to make a scarf for her teddy bear. Toni didn't know what she was going to make. Whatever it was, it was going to look odd. They only had odd bits of wool so their knitting had many different colours in it.

Mum heard a loud knock on the door and got up to answer it. A lady a Gentleman and two children were shown into the room. 'Oh no!' Lizzy thought to herself, 'not more people to live in our house! Someone will be sleeping in the shed next.'
Mum brought the visitors in and introduced them.
"This is Mr and Mrs Braithwaite and their two children, Tom and Maureen."

Toni stopped knitting; she felt her heart give a sudden thump that stuck in her throat. Her legs seemed to have frozen stiff for a moment, unable to move.

Little Maureen was about five or six years old. She held her mother's hand and was smiling. The boy Tom was older: he was on the other side, next to his Dad. He did not seem interested in Toni; his eyes were darting round the room, taking the whole scene in.

Mrs Braithwaite began to speak.
"My name is Edna Braithwaite and this is my husband Tom. We saw the article about Toni in the paper last night, so we just had to try and get in touch. The sergeant at the police station told us to come here. I hope you do not mind, but I do not think there are any other 'Braithwaite's' living around here."

"I was born in Burnley," Mr Braithwaite was saying, Toni could not mistake his northern accent. "My dad worked in the mines..."

In her mind, Toni started to finish his sentence, '...then he had a bad accident. Many miners were seriously injured and so the family moved down here to find different work ...' She had heard this story many times before.

Mr. Braithwaite was looking at Toni; there was something about her he seemed to recognise. Her eyes looked similar to Maureen's, and the way her nose wrinkled when she smiled, it was all very familiar.
"My old dad used to work for Mr Groves, a farmer who lives just on the edge of the village. He is getting on a bit now and can't manage much of the work, so I practically run the whole place for him."
Mrs Braithwaite interrupted her husband.
"It means that Tom here won't be called up to serve in the army. They call it a 'reserved occupation.' We need people to stay behind and run the farms or else there would be nothing

for anyone to eat." Edna said, although she looked rather worried.

"You never know what will happen," Tom was talking, "At my last revue the conscription board agreed they would give me another six months, but since then we have been given four of those land army girls."

"Have they taken over the running of the farm?" Toni asked.

"Not exactly Toni, you see the sight of those four pretty young ladies has put such a spring back in the step of old Mr. Groves that he is running around the place like some kind of spring chicken. Once the authorities realise he can cope they will have me off in the army!"

"That sounds terrible, I bet you are not looking forward to it," Toni remarked.

"To be honest, I would be happy to join up. It has not been easy being at home while all of my mates are doing their bit for the country. Sometimes I can hear tongues wagging behind my back, I know they think that I am a shirker, but I am just as keen as anyone else to help us to win this dreadful war. Is your dad in the army Toni?"

"I don't know," Toni murmured sounding distant now, "I don't know anything about my family. I don't know where they are or what they are doing."

Lizzy's Mum spoke. "Poor Toni has been badly affected by an exploding bomb. She doesn't remember anything about her family. The address she gave doesn't exist; she led one of the police to an empty field."

"Poor lamb!" Mrs Braithwaite sighed, "Come and stand next to our Maureen, Toni." Toni stood up and did as she was told. "The resemblance is quite uncanny, they could practically be sisters!"
Lizzy's Mum nodded her head; the two children were practically identical. They even combed their fringes in the same way.

It took Toni a while to finally realise that she was standing next to her Great Aunt Mo and that the boy standing next to her must be her own grand pa Tom! Tom even had that tiny scar that she would always remember just under his nose.

Toni wanted to race over and hug her grandpa! How often they had walked together holding hands, talking about anything and everything. Toni loved her Grandfather. She couldn't believe he was there now, and aged only seven too!

Great Aunt Maureen had a black smudge on her face where she had scratched her nose with a dirty finger. Toni smiled, she wanted to get the corner of a handkerchief and rub the mark away vigorously, just as her Aunty had often done to her.

Lizzy's Mum was speaking again.
"Why don't you two take Tom and Maureen out for a while? I am sure they don't want to be cooked up inside with the grown-ups all afternoon."

Lizzy thought that was a good idea, soon the four of them were walking down the street towards the park. Maureen was holding Toni tightly by the hand. Tom was walking slightly behind the other three, because he did not really want to be seen with girls!

Maureen stopped and pointed at the clouds. "Toni." She asked in a confused voice, "Why are there Elephants in the sky?"

Toni wondered at Lizzy, "Elephants, what elephants, there aren't any elephants in the sky!"

"Yes there are! Look!" Maureen sounded positive.

Toni and Lizzy looked to where she was pointing. At the end of the street in the far distance they knew there was an important munitions factory. Huge, black, barrage balloons hung in the sky all round the factory.

"They are big balloon things; they stop the enemy planes from trying to fly low and hit the factory."

"But they have ears!" Maureen insisted.

As a gust of wind spun a balloon round, Toni could see the tail flop to one side. Maureen was right. There were Elephants in the sky!"

Tom wasn't listening to anything the girls were talking about. He had climbed up on a wall and was trying to walk along the top of it.

"Tom! Be careful the top of the wall looks un ..."

Lizzy did not speak quickly enough; the block Tom was standing on was lose. It crumbled away as Tom's foot landed on it, sending him tumbling onto the floor.

Tom was lying in a helpless heap, holding his knee and crying loudly. Toni was first on the scene. There was a deep cut on his knee she held it closed with her handkerchief. Between the three of them, they eventually helped poor Tom to limp his miserable way back to the house.

Chapter Twelve
The Braithwaites

By the time Toni had practically carried her grandfather back to his parents, 'decisions' had been made. Mr and Mrs Braithwaite had been firm in their opinion. Toni was obviously a member of their family. She had the same name and was very like their own children. It did not matter to them no one knew who exactly she was; she was going to stay with them in Nuther village.

Mrs Gregg was saying she did not mind keeping Toni with her. They only had one daughter and she had become good friends with Lizzy. Mrs Braithwaite tried to put her foot down. Toni should come home with her. They had a fairly large house in the countryside away from any bombing. Toni would be able to have a room to herself and would be a great help looking after the younger two.

Mrs Gregg decided to let Toni decide. It was only fair, she thought, the poor girl should be the one to choose. Toni was quite amazed; it didn't take her long to make up her mind, although there were one or two conditions which took the family by surprise.

Toni hoped she would be able to come and see Lizzy sometimes. She was sure she would like to play with her occasionally. She also wanted to be able to go to the same school. She did not want to move away from Almund School.

"But Almund School has been closed because of the bombing!" Edna Braithwaite explained, "I am sure there is a school nearer for you."

Toni thought for a moment. "Alright, I will go to a nearby school, it would be boring to have to stay at home all day, but as soon as Almund School opens again, I want to go back there."

Tom Braithwaite senior had the solution to the problem. "You will have to learn to ride my old bike then! I have had it since I was practically your age, it needs fixing up a bit but it should do."

"But it's a boy's bike! How can you expect a girl to ride it? What would people say if they saw her?" Edna sounded concerned.

"I will tell them to mind their own business. After all, there is a war on!" Toni announced, smiling at the thought of being able to ride a bike again.

It was only a short bus journey to the Braithwaite's house. Toni sat at the back of the bus on the long bench seat between Tom and Maureen. Older Tom and Edna sat opposite them, Edna clutching a stiff brown paper parcel containing the only possessions Toni had in the world.

Toni had to hide the smile on her face when they arrived at Tom and Edna's house. She recognised it immediately. When Edna took her by the hand saying, "Let me take you up to the room that is going to be yours." She felt her heart begin to leap with excitement. The stairs were the same, though they were not as rickety as she could remember. The brown carpet was different too, but the pale green painted walls were correct in every detail. That is apart from the huge chunk of plaster she removed when she tried to slide down the stairs on a tea tray aged seven! Toni patted the spot as she climbed the stairs.

The bathroom was not there! It was a small room in which Edna kept her sewing machine. Toni had seen the machine once before when she was rummaging through the attic for some Christmas decorations.

She guessed where the toilet was! Through a window, she could see Tom heading down the garden with a newspaper clutched under his arm. It was going to be cold venturing out there in the middle of the night.

"I do hope you like this room, we keep it for any visitors we have."

Toni was delighted to be back in her own room again. How many school holidays had she spent there while her Mum and Dad were busy at work? How many weekends had they visited, so her Mum could do some house work for ageing Tom and Martha his wife.

Toni giggled to herself, little Tom was running down in the garden to find his dad, probably to complain there were far too many girls in the house.

Toni couldn't help clapping her hands in delight as she saw the bed pushed under the window. There was a fireplace where Grandpa Tom had lit a fire for her once, when she had spent a week in bed with a bout of 'flu.

It was just as it should be, though the yellow paint on the walls did not seem to have faded quite so much as Toni recalled.

Toni reached out a hand to switch on the bedroom light, but there was nothing there, then she saw a stub of dripping candle on a little bedside table. Perhaps there was no electric light upstairs here either, just like in Lizzy's house.

Toni sat on the bed her feet dangling above the floor. There was something else she could remember about the room. The loose floorboard! Under the bed, next to the corner of the room there was a loose piece of floorboard. It was about a foot long. Toni had discovered it one wet afternoon when she had been playing in her room. There was a small space when the board was lifted out. A special place where she used to hide biscuits and toffee ready for a midnight feast!

Toni remembered her green owl. It had been her lucky owl, but now it was lost. It had vanished when the bomb exploded. This was where she had found it. It had been left by someone under the floorboards. Toni had found it when she lifted the board for the first time. She did not know who had put it there, or to whom it belonged.

Toni scrambled under the bed to see if the board was still there. It didn't take her long to find it, but the hole was empty. The owl wasn't there after all.

"Come down to the kitchen dear," Edna had suggested, "when you have put your things away I will make us all a nice hot cup of tea."

The kitchen! Toni had quite forgotten about that. It should have a big black cast iron range. The handles of the doors would be made of brass and polished so they gleamed. The fire door would be open and within hot coals glowed red. The kettle was always on, ready to make tea at a moment's notice.

Toni hurried down stairs and burst into the kitchen.

"I was going to leave the door open so you would know which room was the kitchen," Edna said, "They all try the back room first, but you seem to have found your bearings quickly."

Toni gazed round the room. The floor was still covered in ancient stone. The walls tiled half way in bottle green. Beyond the tiles the thick plaster was white washed. A row of brass jugs hung from a beam over the fire.

Two small pipes stuck out of the wall with small glass globes on them. Toni wondered what they were, and then she remembered being shown where the old gas lights used to be. It was just like stepping back in time. This was exactly what she had done.

Mr. Braithwaite was on his way up the garden with young Tom in his shadow. She noticed they were carrying something large and heavy, and they were bringing it into the kitchen.

Chapter Thirteen
Dig For Victory

"Those slugs must be on Hitler's side!" Old Tom was saying, "Just look at the mess they have made of our cabbages. Some of them just have a few stalks sticking out of the ground!"

"I've never seen a goose-stepping slug before!" Toni said.

Young Tom held out a decimated leaf for inspection. There were huge holes in every leaf and tiny silvery trails showed the slugs' path to lunch.

"It's a shame Tom," Edna sighed, "They were looking so good a few days ago too!"

Edna spooned some tea into the pot. Tom didn't need to ask.

Toni did not know why but she suddenly found herself joining in the conversation.

"Have you tried garlic?" She asked.

"Garlic, Oh no, hate the stuff, make my breath smell like an old sock!"

"No, I don't mean to eat," Toni laughed, "We used to boil some crushed garlic in a pan for about an hour or so and then strain it off and use the water to spray the cabbages."

Tom was all ears.

"Does it work?"

"Yes! It really does, I think the slugs hate the taste of garlic just as much as you do, and they keep right off."

"That would work so long as they are not Italian slugs!" Tom suggested.

"If you think you are boiling some garlic up in a pan in my kitchen you have another thing coming. The whole house will reek of it for days!" Edna was emphatic.

"Me and the girl here will light a fire at the end of the garden and do it down there. Sounds like the best idea I have heard of since cabbages turned green!"

Toni loved the way he called her 'the girl'. She guessed this simple idea had made them friends for ever.

"You could put copper bands round the cabbages too, slugs don't like that either."

Tom gave her one of his stern looks, "I don't think they would take too kindly to me using copper in the garden. It's needed for them aeroplanes and stuff."

Toni nodded her head in agreement, her suggestion wasn't appropriate during a war.

"I even tried filling some old jars with a bit of beer to try and catch them. Waste of good beer if you ask me though!"

"My dad would agree!" Toni smiled. "My dad told me something that my grandfather did."

"What was that Toni?"

"Well, apparently he wanted to grow some tomatoes, but he couldn't get any seeds because the shops didn't have any in. So off he went to the greengrocers and asked if he could buy a tomato!"

"A tomato?"

"Yes! Just the one. The man behind the counter asked him if he was very poor, but Grandfather said he would have half a tomato if he would sell it to him"

Old Tom was smiling now.

"So back home he went with his half a tomato, he cut it up and scraped the seeds out and dried them on an old bit of blotting paper he had! Then he grew his tomatoes from those seeds!"

Old Tom was suddenly staring at Toni.

"And your dad told you that story Toni?"

"Yes he did, he thought it was very funny." Toni noticed the confused expression on Tom's face.

"I don't understand it," Tom exclaimed, "That story you just told: it's exactly what I did last year!"

Toni felt her heart go thump; she would have to be very careful about what she told Tom.

"I can't believe your Grandfather did the exact same trick as me!" Toni was looking the other way; she did not dare to look him in the eyes.

"Where is your Dad?" Tom said changing the subject, "Is he away with the forces?"

Toni was unhappy. "I don't know. I don't know anything. They could be anywhere. I have lost them all."

Tom put an arm round her shoulder.

"Don't you worry girl, they will be out there looking for you. Once that memory of yours comes back things will be different. Just let it take its own time."

Toni held his hand; he seemed to know there was something different about her, but she knew he was going to keep very quiet about it.

The kettle on the black range began to sing. Toni watched as Edna carefully began to fill a tea pot, making sure an open oven door in the range was not accidentally pushed shut.

"You haven't seen her have you?" Edna asked, noticing Toni's interest, "come and have a look."

Edna opened the door a bit more,

"There is a cat in the oven!" Toni exclaimed, "Wont she get burnt?"

"It's not a proper hot oven dear. It's just for warming plates or letting bread rise. Mrs Cat thinks it's her personal bedroom."

Toni watched as Mrs Cat wrapped her tail round her head. She was totally black; exactly the same colour as Edna's huge cooking range. Toni could see Mrs Cat had one white smudge near her ear. Edna explained a big dog had grabbed Mrs Cat by the ear a while ago and the hair had turned white on the scar.

"It is so hard to see her!" Toni questioned, "Does she ever get shut in by accident?"

"That would be a terrible thing to happen so we always make sure she is safe. I can't remember when I last closed the door."

"Or warmed any plates!" Tom grumbled. "The cat rules round here."

Tom and Toni sat side by side on a bench next to the wall. The kitchen table pushed up against them. Edna placed a cup of tea in front of them both.

"What's with the cups, Edna! Toni here is family. Get out the jam jars we usually use!"

Edna made to flick a tea towel at him, but he knew what was coming and ducked out of the way.

"What sort of garden do you have then?" Tom asked.

Toni didn't know what to say: the only proper vegetable growing garden she had ever been in was just beyond Tom's back door.

"We just have a plot at the bottom of the garden. My grandfather grows just about all the vegetables we need."

"Sounds like he knows what he is doing. I could do with his help here. Some of my onions have just run to seed!"

There was a lengthy discussion about onions and cabbages, carrots and peas, it ended with the two of them walking down the garden, side by side, so they could have a better look at the problems Tom was having to deal with.

There was one bed raised up from the surrounding ground by a few old railway sleepers.

"What's that for?" Toni asked.

"Carrot fly," Tom replied, "There are these white flies, they eat the tops of carrots and damage them. I found the flies cannot fly more than a few feet up in the air so I plant my carrots in a raised bed to keep the flies away from them."

"Does it work?"

"Sort of, though I think if there is a strong breeze they get blown there anyway."

"We usually plant a row of marigolds with the carrots. Someone told my dad the smell keeps white flies away."

"Edna would like that, she gets fed up with just having vegetables in the garden, she would love to see a few flowers too."

Toni could see a few wooden nesting boxes nailed to the trees.

"You like birds too?"

"Not bothered really, but I thought if I can get them to nest close to my cabbages then maybe they will pick off any caterpillars hatched out on them."

"Good idea!"

When Toni told him a few more of her special tips, Tom stroked his chin and added, "You know, I thought I was the only one who had ever thought of doing things like that!"

Toni had to smile, because he probably was!

There were few flowers growing in Tom's garden, just some straggling roses, which clung to the back door frame for comfort.

"This patch was Edna's flower bed before the war!" Tom told her, "but we dug it up to plant onions and leeks."

Toni was going to ask why, but she didn't need to.

"We can't eat flowers; there is a war on. Mr Churchill says we have to dig for victory. She can have her flowers back when the Hitler bloke is six foot under!"

Toni had to agree.

"And if they want to pop him in my garden, it's alright by me. I bet my rhubarb will make a good show if it ever gets its teeth into the likes of him!"

Toni and Tom returned to the house with more offerings for the table. Tom had dug up a bucket full of large potatoes and Toni carried an armful of creamy parsnips, there might be rationing in all the shops but no one was going to go hungry thanks to Tom's efforts.

Chapter Fourteen
Nuver School

If Edna had thought that suggesting Toni went the village school would be met with complaining, she couldn't have been more wrong. Toni missed school, she loved reading and writing. She endured Maths too because it often led to other, more interesting tasks.

"You will like our Miss Booth. She looks a bit odd, but she has a heart of gold."

"Miss Booth?" Toni thought she had heard her name somewhere before.

Nuver School had been designed as a village school where the children from the surrounding farms and cottages could be educated. There were only two rooms, one for the Infants and one for the Juniors. They shared playgrounds and toilets. For the two teachers it was an idyllic situation. They knew all the local families and over the years the two ladies had probably taught most of the people living in and around the village to read and write.

The school's head teacher was a Miss Booth. She had never married; her intended husband having sadly been killed during the First World War. This was why she always wore black, in solemn mourning for her loss. She cut a strange and rather forbidding figure. The only adornment she allowed into her life was a circular pendant which hung around her neck, its bright silver complementing her black attire. She was never without it because it had been a final present from her missing 'intended'. Miss Booth gathered in her flock as if they were her own, substituting the children from the farms and villages for the happy family she might once have had.

The happy land, where no more than ten or twelve children had run around in the playground was in the past. Days when the whole school took a picnic down to the stream had gone. Nature walks in the woods, where older pupils held the hands of younger ones as they searched for squirrels and badgers, were no more. Since the day war had been declared, life for the village teachers had taken a huge turn for the worse.

The school was packed to the door. The number of children attending Nuver School had gone up overnight, from a 'tinkling twelve' to an outrageous 'one hundred and twenty, 'as evacuees from the big cities arrived by the train load, all seeking safety and refuge, away from the bombing of the blitz.

Miss Dobson and Miss Booth cowered in the corner of their classrooms. Their fragile lives turned upside down in an instant. They did not feel ready for the onslaught that would surely burst through the doors once they dared to pull the rope to ring the bell on the school roof.

Edna had walked to school with Toni, concerned her charge should be installed comfortably but without undue fuss. Maureen held onto Toni's hand, but Tom walked on the other side of his mother, embarrassed to be near the girls.

The family reached the school gate to find a crowd of children with a few harassed mothers, watching helplessly as a fight took place. The women were wondering who was going to be first to dare to intervene and break up the fight between two boys. Fists flew, punches landed and kicks were swung. Blood trickled from one nostril but it did not stop the continued attack. The whole school crowded round, shouting encouragement and pushing the pugilists closer.

Edna had seen enough. "Stay there children!" she exclaimed, and off she went into the middle of the fray, only to emerge seconds later with a boy dangling from each hand.
"Billy Wilkins!" She shouted, "What is the meaning of this! We are fighting the Germans, not each other."
Billy Wilkins snivelled.
"What will your mother say when I tell her?"
"It's him, Mrs Braithwaite; he called us a 'load of carrot crunchers'."

Edna looked at the other boy sternly, she didn't recognise him and he was new round here.
"And what, may I ask, is your name?"
The boy spat on the floor and remained silent.
"I asked you what your name was young man?"
He spat on the floor again and rubbed it in with his foot.
"You can't do nothing to ...Ow!"
The sudden sting from the clip across his ear which Edna had expertly delivered, made him cower.
"There is plenty more where that came from! Now what is your name?"

He was crying now. "You hit me, I am telling my dad!"

"Tell him!" Edna whispered, "Bring your Mum, your uncle Fred, his dog and next door's cat too. I don't mind. Now what is your name?"

Miss Booth arrived, not before time.

"Oh Mrs Braithwaite, lovely to see you, how are you these days. And who is this darling young lady, a new addition to our growing throng?"

"I found these two fighting like savages. I will see Billy's mother later. If you have any bother from the other one just let me know, it's been a while since my hand got any proper exercise! "

"Oh I don't think that will be necessary Mrs Braithwaite, Kevin here has only just arrived. Once he knows who is boss he will soon settle down."

Edna didn't look so sure.

Toni was a little taken aback. Miss Booth was wearing gloves made from some kind of black lace. She looked down at the teacher's feet, wondering if this lady was really one of Roald Dahl's Witches she had read about. Miss Booth seemed to be a very kindly lady, surely she wasn't about to change anyone into a mouse.

For most of the morning session, Toni sat in a corner with a book, reading quietly to herself. Miss Dobson kept herself in the Infants room, only venturing out to retrieve a wandering child.

In contrast to Miss Booth, Miss Dobson was dressed in a very bright sunny dress belted tightly to emphasise her waspish waistline. Toni wasn't sure, but she thought the large shoulder pads were very silly; they made her look like Batman's assistant!

Miss Dobson didn't like her domain to be interrupted or ventured into by any outsiders. Everyone could see she was having a terrible time coping with all the extra children, but she refused to accept help from anyone, even though offers were often forthcoming.

At playtime Toni stood by the railings, munching and apple Edna had picked straight off the tree for her.
"Hey you! New girl! What have you got?" A boy sloped up to her. He didn't look very clean and his nose dribbled alarmingly.
"Just an apple, that's all."
"Have you got any toffee or cough drops?"
"No, I haven't sorry."
"That's not good enough, new girl." He came a bit closer, grabbing hold of the collar of her dress in his rough hand. "I am in charge round here, in case you didn't know!"
"Oh I am sorry I didn't." Toni tried to sound interested.
"So you do what I tell you to, right?"
"I do what you tell me to do?" Toni was puzzled.
"You can start by bringing me sixpence tomorrow, right!"
"I am sorry I haven't got any money. I don't have a sixpence."
"The woman you are with has got plenty; get it from her purse if you know what is good for you!"
"You want me to steal some money and give it to you?"
"You learn quickly, I am in charge around here, so you do as I say. Got it?"

Toni was totally flustered, the boy let go of her collar, leaving a dark smudge where his thumb had been and went off to find his next victim.

Toni was having none of this! She went straight away to find Miss Booth and let her know one of her charges was going round the playground, demanding money with menaces!

"You mean Arnold over there? He comes from Southampton poor lamb. His mother wrote to me last week. It was a lovely letter: she wanted to be sure no one was bullying her boy."

"It's the other way round!" Toni argued.

"He is such a sad boy; he must feel so out of place in this little school coming from such a big city! I am sure he will settle down eventually."

Back in the classroom Arnold sat in a corner of his own, looking at the pictures in a comic. When asked to put it away and begin his work, he just turned his back and made rude noises. Miss Booth was not going to get much from him.

Nuver School was only a stone's throw from the Braithwaite's house so Toni ambled back there when the school was dismissed for dinner.

Tom was home from work for his lunch too. He had a surprise for Edna. He placed a brace of rabbits on the draining board.

"Here you go Edna! A pair of beauties for you!"

The rabbits' eyes were wide open, as if they had been suddenly and finally startled by something.

"His Lordship up at the house bagged them this morning. He's heard we had an extra mouth to feed, so passed them my way."

"That's kind of him Tom; I must remember to thank him when I see him after church on Sunday."

Toni looked at the two fluffy bunnies, lying side by side, their little white tails smeared with their own blood. She gently stroked the pair with her hand, fearing it was going to be impossible for her to eat anything that had once been so gorgeous.

Soon the family were tucking into a Woolton Pie Edna had made.

"Mr Braithwaite," Toni ventured, "There is a boy at school who is trying to make me steal money from Mrs Braithwaite's purse. You have both been kind to me. I would never do that to you!"

"Who is this lout?" Tom asked.

"I think he is called Arnold, he is from Southampton. He told me I had to do as he said 'or else'."

"He did, did he? So what are you going to do about him, girl?"

"Well I am not going to steal anything! I told Miss Booth, but she wasn't interested."

Tom gave her a gentle kiss on the forehead.

"You will have to sort him out for yourself then. It won't take much, just stand up to him, bully's are like that. They only go after someone they think is weaker than they are. If you could punch straight, he would run away!"

The Woolton Pie was delicious. There wasn't any meat in it, just carrots, parsnips and onions inside a thick pastry Edna had made with potatoes. It had a little grated cheese on top, but the best part was the thick vegetable gravy.

Toni remembered turning her nose up at the menu for her school's party. It might have been alright after all, but no one would have been able to cook like Edna.

Back in the playground, Arnold was waiting for her. He held out his hand demanding the sixpence he wanted.

"Not here!" Toni explained, trying to look her most humble and pathetic, "Meet me round the corner by the bins. I don't want anyone to see me."

Arnold seemed satisfied; a new victim would be added to the growing list. He followed Toni as she walked round the corner.

He held out his hand again. This was all Toni needed; those Judo lessons in the school hall had not been for nothing. Before he realised what was happening Arnold was lying on his back on the stony ground. Toni had her foot on his neck and had begun twisting his arm. Anymore and the pain would be unbearable.

"I don't have sixpence!" Toni glared at him, "but you can have a four penny one if you like?"

Arnold started to cry. "You are hurting me! Get off!"

Toni let go of his hand and watched as the bully scrambled to his feet. He was not going to let a girl get away with that.

A fist flew through the air; Toni ducked to the side to avoid it and grabbed the hand as it passed. It was strange how things seemed to fit exactly into place. For a moment or two she was back in her old school. The Judo coach was talking them though an 'Ippon Seoinage' or 'shoulder throw' as she called it.

Amy had lunged towards her so, using the force of her movement and her shoulder, Toni had thrown her flat on her back on the mat. This time however, there was no mat and it wasn't her friend Amy.

 It was Arnold and a pile of metal dustbins. He landed with a clatter that sent Toni's ears ringing.

"Looser!" Toni exclaimed as she dusted her hands together and headed back to the play ground.

Chapter Fifteen
Potatoes

The afternoon lessons began with Arnold sitting at the back of the class, still snivelling quietly to himself. Toni eyed him dangerously as she walked past him towards her place. She purposely dropped a book on the floor and whispered in his ear.

"If I ever catch you taking money from any of the other children in this school, you will find yourself dumped over the railings! Now get on with your work and pay attention to Miss Booth."

The children were all sat in pairs and in rows behind heavy wooden desks. Some children sat three to a desk but, being new, Toni was given a little more space so she could settle in.

"Who can tell me what this is?" Miss Booth asked, holding up a large, blackened object. A hand went up at the back of the class.

"Yes Gordon?"

"Is it a Maris Piper?"

There were howls of laughter from all round the room.

"Stupid carrot cruncher: anyone can see it's a spud!"

Miss Booth smiled, "Gordon lives on a farm; he knows it is a potato. He also knows it's a variety of potato that is popular called 'Maris Piper', so in many ways, you are both right."

Gordon was a quite smug.

"Now who can tell me where this potato comes from?"

"We get ours from Stanley's Miss, he always has them in."

"My Mum goes to the market on Wednesdays and gets them from a stall."

These answers prompted more questions.

"But where does the shop man or the market stall get potatoes from?" Miss Booth waited for someone to speak. The local village children had decided to remain silent.

"Stanley gets them delivered Miss, they come in sacks."

There were nods of agreement all round the room.

A girl put her hand up: she had something to say.

"The lady I am with told me she needed some spuds. I thought she would have to wait until the morning because all the shops would be shut in the evening. Then she told me to get a big bucket and follow her. So I got the bucket and she picked up a spade and we went down the garden."

Everyone was listening. "Do carry on Mildred." Miss Booth encouraged.

"Well we went down the garden, it was getting late and it was just starting to get dark. She got the spade and dug it into the dirty soil. Up came a lot of black things just like the one you have got. She claimed they were potatoes! I knew she was lying; they were dirty and had worms on them. There was no way I was eating them!"

Some children made noises and pretended to be sick.

Billy spoke up too.

"It happens where I live. They dig up carrots too. Round here they don't have any proper spuds or anything; everything they eat comes out of the soil. It looks bad. I won't eat it either!

They should get some shops round here, and then we would have proper spuds and carrots and stuff!"

The class all agreed and started talking about the shops they got their food from back home. A few children who had remained silent were smiling to themselves. Miss Booth was looking at them trying to get them to say something too.

"All potatoes come from the ground." Miss Booth explained.
"No they don't, they come from shops in sacks!"
"Yes they do!" Toni exclaimed, "Don't you know anything?"
"Carrot cruncher!!" A boy stared at her.
"Whatever!" Toni ignored him.
"Where does the shop get them from? Who puts them in the sacks?"

A voice finally dared to speak. "Last year when they were ready, me and my brother went to help our dad with the harvest. He dug the potatoes up with his tractor and then we put them into sacks!"
There were unbelieving faces all round the room.
"What happened to the sacks?"
"There were lots and lots of sacks: a big lorry came and took them away. My dad told me they were taking them to the market."

"You mean to tell me the spuds we get at home come from here. They come out of the dirty ground?"

Miss Booth breathed a sigh of relief. At last she was getting through to some of the new children. They came from the big cities and had no idea where the food they ate came from.

"I am never eating potatoes again!" Billy affirmed. Lots of other children groaned in agreement.

"Then you are all being silly," Miss Booth told the class. "Our Mr Churchill wants us all to work hard and dig for victory. He wants us to plant seeds and grow as much of our own food as we can. We cannot rely on our food coming to us from farms in other countries. Mr Hitler has sent nasty submarines to sink the ships that bring food to us, so we have to start growing our own."

"My dad was on a ship when it got sunk by a torpedo; he had to stay in a lifeboat for three days until he was rescued."

"This is why Miss Dobson and I have decided we are going to dig up part of our school field and start to grow our own potatoes and carrots. If it all goes right, we shall try and grow other vegetables too."

"I hate cabbage Miss; I don't want to grow any cabbages."

"Or sprouts Miss, I hate them too."

"I don't like them onion things. I vote we don't grow them either."

A row broke out in class. Half of the children liked what the other half hated. They could not agree on anything.

"Miss, since there are no sweets in the shops now, could we please grow some chocolate instead?"

"Oh yes! Please Miss can we?... Please Miss, oh go on Miss, say yes!"

There was shouting and screaming all around the room. Children stood up on their desks so they could be heard. In the middle, Miss Booth tried to remain calm, but Toni could tell she was getting to the end of her tether.

When the bell finally rang the children charged for the door eager to be out in the open air once more. Miss Booth slumped over her desk wondering why a simple lesson about potatoes had gone so wrong. She was glad she was teaching in a little village school: life in the towns must be dreadful, if these children were anything to go by.

Edna was waiting for Toni by the school gates. She had young Tom in one hand and little Maureen in the other. Tom had been rescued from Miss Dobson's class. Maureen was, of course, still too young to go to school.

Chapter Sixteen
Owl

"It's a nice afternoon," Edna told her, "I thought it might be nice to take a walk into the woods for a few minutes on our way home and see if we can find any mushrooms: they would be nice to have for tea if we can find them."

Toni watched as the school children vanished down the village main street. It was just as well Miss Booth didn't tell them about mushrooms, she thought; some of them would only have gone picking the wrong ones and poisoned themselves.

Little Tom ran ahead and found a stick which he turned into a Tommy gun. As they walked along the path leading to the woods, 'commando Tom' leapt out from behind trees and bushes, to confront his enemy with rapid fire.

Maureen held tightly to her mother's hand, she had heard there were bears and wolves living in the woods, along with cottages made of ginger bread and trees that watched with angry faces. She was staying where it was safe, close to her Mum.

Toni held the wicker basket Edna had brought and began searching for the white gems she had seen so often on supermarket shelves.
"Be careful!" Edna warned, "Sometimes something that looks just like a mushroom can be deadly poisonous. Don't let

Maureen or Tom near anything, especially Tom; he will only try to eat it right here!"

Edna told her there probably wouldn't be any mushrooms growing in the woods. The best place to look for them was on the edge of the fields, where the woods began. So they left the woodland path and climbed over a gate into a farmer's field.

Maureen found a ring of toadstools growing among the grass.

"Look Maureen," Toni explained, taking the little girl by the hand," This is where the fairies dance in the moonlight."

Maureen began to dance and skip round the circle too, taking care not to damage any of the fairies toadstool homes. Then she collected some tiny twigs and dried grass stalks.

"I am helping the fairies. I am collecting wood so they will be warm at night." Maureen left tiny piles of sticks next to some of the larger toadstools, so the fairies would find them.

Tom was crawling in the grass, pretending he was creeping up on some Germans.

Maureen shouted for him to be careful, he was getting too near her fairy friends. He was also getting close to a smelly pat a lonely cow had left behind. Next to it, there was a large white fungus about as big as a large tennis ball.

"Is this one alright?" Toni asked.

"I don't think so! It looks a bit too big for me: it could be a wrong one."

Toni was glum; she thought one that size would make a whole meal on its own.

It wasn't long before Toni got the hang of it and didn't need to keep asking Edna to check what she was picking. With a good basketful of mushrooms, Edna turned and a headed towards home. Toni wanted to pick more, but Edna thought they should only take what they needed for themselves. There wouldn't be many next time if they cleared every single mushroom away.

Something caught Toni's eye. It seemed to stand out among the roots of a tree. Toni bent down to see what it was. She had to sweep away many layers of accumulated leaves before the whole object was revealed.

Toni could not believe what she was holding in her hand. It was a green owl. It had been carved out of some kind of soft stone and had a hole at the top that would turn it into a pendant.

'*It's my owl!*' Toni cried to herself, '*I lost it when the bomb exploded! Now here it is, lying in the middle of these woods: how it can be?*'

Edna called her back to her senses.

"What have you got there, Toni? Have you found something?"

Toni showed her the owl, holding it out in her hand so Edna could see it more clearly.

"That is a lucky find. Someone must have been sad to lose it! If we ask Tom, he might find you a thin piece of string or leather, and then you can wear it round your neck."

Toni nodded. It sounded like a wonderful idea.

"We will have to clean it up first though, it looks mucky!"

"This will be my lucky charm!" Toni declared, "I was lucky to find it and I'm sure it will bring me some good luck."

On their way home Toni carried the basket of mushrooms while Edna held tightly to Tom and Maureen. The sky was starting to darken and she did not want to lose sight of them. On the corner by the village school Toni saw an old man hobbling along towards them. He was wearing an ancient black suit and seemed to be lost in his own thoughts.

"That's Reverend Thomas," Edna knew him. "He is the vicar in our church. We must say hello to him."

Rev. Thomas smiled broadly when he saw the three children with Edna.

"And who may I ask is this young lady?" he asked, as soon as they were close enough to talk.

Edna told him the story about how Toni had come to live with her and Tom.

"You are both generous and kind," he told Edna, "If there is one good thing this terrible war has done, it's to bring out the good in everyone. I hope it will continue when the war is over. Though I doubt we will ever be happy again if the Germans succeed with their evil conquest."

"They won't succeed, they will be defeated, and Hitler will be no more." Toni found herself saying.

"You seem certain of that fact young lady. Have you got some inside information that you are party to?"

Toni wanted to tell him he need not worry, but she decided to quickly change the subject. Rev. Thomas was obviously a man not easily fooled.

"I found this," Toni announced, showing Rev. Thomas her strange owl. "It was lying under the roots of a tree; it looks like it had been there a long time."

Rev. Thomas took a pair of wire rimmed spectacles from his pocket and began to examine the owl.

"This is an interesting find Toni. If I am not mistaken, I think it may have been lying in the ground for much longer than you realise."

Toni gasped.

"Long ago the Romans and the Greeks had the same god, the Romans called her Minerva: the Greeks called her Athena. She was an important god and her symbol was an owl. The Romans used to carry owl charms to help them. I think this may well be a Roman owl. It could be around two thousand years old!"

Toni's eyes spread wide.

"Come to the vicarage tomorrow after school and bring your owl with you. I have some books in my study which might help us to identify it."

Toni was on the point of suggesting they could look it up on the Internet, but realised quickly how silly her suggestion would be.

Chapter Seventeen
Brenda

With over fifty children of all different ages in her room, Miss Booth was finding life difficult. There were a few children who could read, but there were many who were struggling to know any letters.

It took most of the next day before Miss Booth finally managed to have a few quick words with Toni. She was surprised to see her newest pupil was sitting quietly reading a fairly thick book.

"What is the book you are reading child?" Miss Booth asked. The silver pendant round her neck jingled on the desk as she leaned forward.

"It's one I brought in from Mrs Braithwaite's house; I found it on a book shelf there. It's good!"

Miss Booth abruptly picked up the book and read the title, 'Treasure Island,' by Robert Louis Stevenson.

"There are some difficult words in this book child, are you sure you can read them all?"

Toni gave her one of her looks.

"Would you like me to read some of it to you, or tell you the story I have read so far?" She asked trying hard not to sound impertinent or bad mannered.

"No, that will be fine. I sometimes find that children gravitate towards large books before they have acquired all the reading skills they need." The silver disk caught a rare ray of sunshine that made Toni blink her eyes.

"I like your silver pendant Miss, it is beautiful!"

"Thank you Toni, it is precious to me. You can look at it if you like."

Toni admired her teacher's necklace. There was an owl in the middle of the disk surrounded with lots of other strange symbols that Toni did not understand.

"I found an owl charm too! It was in the woods, Miss! Rev Thomas thinks it might be Roman: he wants me to call in at the vicarage and let him see it. He has some books about Roman things."

Miss Booth was very interested

"Rev Thomas is a wonderful man; he explained things to me too. The Owl is supposed to be a symbol of wisdom and those other things around my pendant are to do with the months of the year. I am glad you find that sort of thing interesting. You seem to understand a lot for your age, and your reading is good too I see."

"Thank you Miss Booth; that is kind of you." Toni had a sudden idea," If you like I could hear some of the other children read. I used to do it at my old school."

Miss Booth was surprised. "I would have thought you would be better occupied with your own studies!"

"My teacher let us help with the younger children. She had the idea that some of them thought reading was only for grownups and if they saw other children enjoying reading, it might help them to enjoy it too."

Miss Booth considered this for a moment or two.

"Under normal circumstances I certainly would not tolerate letting someone untrained and inexperienced lose in my classroom. However, these are not normal times. If you think you can help with reading, then I would welcome your assistance in the matter."

Toni was directed towards a desk where two girls were sat together.

Toni crouched down beside the two girls.
Sue seemed to be plodding along with her book at a slow pace, but Brenda's eyes were lost in space.

"What's the matter?" Toni asked kindly, "is the book a little too hard for you?"

"The book is alright," Brenda answered," I was thinking about something else."

Toni noticed Brenda's eyes, she could see that tears were starting to well up in them, and then a large drop splashed onto her book. Brenda screwed up her eyes trying to hold back the tears but it was no use, they just had to come.

Toni put a friendly arm around Brenda's shoulders, "if there is something upsetting you, you have to tell someone."

"It's no use; there is nothing that can be done. I was just missing my Mum that is all. It has been ages since I saw her."

Toni felt a lump in her own throat; it had been a long time since she had seen her Mum too.

"Where is she?" Toni asked.

"I don't know, our house was destroyed by a German bomb, I don't know where my Mum is now."

Brenda noticed Toni was wearing something round her neck; she could see the leather strip.

"What is it?" She asked.

"It is my Owl, I was lucky; I found it when I was in the woods looking for mushrooms with Edna."

Toni got it out and let Brenda hold it.

"If it is lucky then maybe it will bring me some luck too," Brenda pressed the Owl between her hands and whispered, "Please, please, please let me see my Mum soon!"

Toni was interested in what Brenda had been saying.

"You were lucky you were not in your house when that bomb dropped on it."

"It didn't land on our house, it landed in the garden."

Brenda started to tell her story.

"I had to go to bed with all of my clothes on, because my Mum thought that there might be an air raid during the night and we would have to go to the shelter."

"It must have been odd having to sleep with your clothes on!"

"She wanted me to sleep with my shoes on too, but I was uncomfortable so I took them off. I must have fallen asleep because I was woken up as sirens swamped the whole town. My grandmother came into the room and shouted for me to hurry up. She shouted, 'Come on, move child! We are not going to a picnic!'

"Then we had to grope our way down the garden path to the shelter. It was so dark. Mr Rankin our neighbour told us we must not put our torches on, or the Germans would see them from their planes and drop bombs right on top of us. We could hear the drone of the enemy planes getting closer so we hurried along. The path was so slippery it was like a skating rink!"

"It must have been scary out there in the dark!"

"We could see the crisscross of the searchlights in the sky, but they did not help us to find our way to the shelter. I was scared, but we finally got there and Mum told me I had to sleep in an old tin bath; then she threw some coats over me."

Toni asked Brenda what it was like.

"I could hear all the grownups sitting round a smelly paraffin stove and talking. There were bunk beds for them to sleep on later and shelves on the side of the shelter with tins of stuff and water if we happened to be stuck down there longer than we had expected to be." Brenda shivered as if she was back in the cold place, and Toni leaned forward to encourage the girl to carry on.

"I must have been dozing under those dusty old coats. Suddenly there was the shock and tremor of an explosion. Everything shook! I was thrown around, but I do not know where. I was very frightened and I couldn't see anything. It seemed ages before I heard the noise of spades grating on metal. I was upside down and I'd become trapped inside the tin bath!"

"Could you tell what the men were saying?"

"They were shouting at my Mum and Grandmother, telling them if they did not leave they would be forcibly removed!"

"Your Mum and Gran must have escaped just as the bomb exploded."

"I could hear the men digging; I could hear their spades scraping the soil. They were saying, 'Is she dead or alive, dead or alive?' Then I was hauled out of the bath and held steady by two air raid wardens."

"You were lucky, that tin bath probably saved you." Toni marvelled.

"That's what the men said. I had always thought being lucky was winning a prize in the lucky dip at the fair ground! Then these men told me to go to another shelter, where I would be safe. They said my Mum and Grandmother would be there waiting for me.

I had to climb over three garden fences because the houses were damaged and I could not go through them. By the time I got to the other shelter, I was covered in cuts and bruises but my Mum and my Grandmother weren't there. I could hear some people shouting at the men to go and look for me when I came in through the door! But it wasn't my Mum and Gran."

Toni wondered what had happened to her mother.

"I kept wondering if it was all real. Was I dead or alive? The bomb had shaken me up so much, I didn't really know. They sent me here to be safe away from the bombing, but I have lost my Mum I don't know where she is. Mum must think I am dead."

Toni put a hand on Brenda's. The poor girl had been through a lot. She needed her Mum even more than Toni needed hers.

Miss Booth came up to find them. Toni thought the teacher was checking up on her, making sure she was doing the job she had been given to do correctly, but she wasn't.

"Brenda dear, put away your book for now. There is a visitor outside waiting to see you!"

Toni stood up and watched as Brenda raced out into the playground into the arms of her mother! Toni glanced down at the owl hanging round her neck; she could not believe Brenda's wish had come true so quickly.

Chapter Eighteen
Rev. Thomas

Toni walked up the driveway to a large, stone-built house that stood right next to the village church. It was one of the biggest houses in the village, so Toni guessed she had got the right one.

Tall trees curved over on either side of the driveway, making Toni feel she was walking down a long tunnel on her way to the vicarage. There were overgrown bushes and piles of dead leaves beyond the trees.

'The vicar does not have much time to spend in his huge garden,' Toni thought. Old Tom would have had most of it dug over and planted with cabbages.

A large wooden door stood in the middle of the front of the building. Toni wanted to see if there was a bell to ring, but all she could see was an old wrought iron knocker, high up in the middle of the door. She had to jump up to reach it.

A young lady, who must have been his housekeeper, showed Toni into Rev Thomas' study. There was a large desk dominating the room, behind it was a tiny window, which let a few rays of light in. The rest of the room was lined with shelves on which Toni could see all manner of books. Most of them seemed important and looked demanding and very difficult to read: they were bound in dark leather with the titles on the book's spines picked out in ancient gold lettering.

Rev. Thomas was sitting in a huge chair, a pair of glasses perched on the end of his nose. The room had a pleasant smell of leather mixed with tobacco; it reminded Toni of her Uncle's house.

"Ah there you are young lady, have you had a busy day at school? Is our Miss Booth keeping you all under control?"

Toni smiled; she preferred not to have to answer that question. Poor Miss Booth had a lot to put up with. There were many more children in the village school than the poor teacher had ever been used to.

"I have been looking through some of my books about the Greeks and I found this picture of Athena for you." Rev. Thomas had one book open on a page for Toni.

"Thank you!" Toni replied, "I love reading about Athena, she has the head of the Gorgon Medusa on her shield and that's Nike the 'Goddess of Victory' in her hand."

Rev. Thomas was astounded. "You are never going to tell me you read those stories in Greek!"

"Oh No! We had some books in school that had lots of information in them. We searched for facts about them on the school's com..."

Toni suddenly stopped speaking. She had nearly let the word 'computer' slip!

"The school's com ... com... compendium of stuff!"

She went bright red; Rev Thomas was obviously going to be asking questions.

"You seem to know a lot about Ancient Greece Toni, I only read the stories when I was learning the Greek language at grammar school. I think I would have loved to have known them when I was your age."

Toni breathed a sigh of relief. He hadn't realised anything.

"Can I have a look at this owl of yours?"

Toni took it from round her neck and handed it over.

"I don't understand how it came to be among the roots of a tree. You told me the owl was probably well over a thousand years old, yet the tree it was stuck in could only be a hundred years old, at most."

"That's an interesting thought Toni. You are quite right. The owl was lying in the ground long before the tree grew. It may not even have been in that spot. The ground gets moved around by people walking, horse's hooves and other animals churning it up. When the owl was dropped, it may have been buried under dead leaves and then forced up through the ground as trees and bushes grew. We just don't know how it came to be there."

"But who dropped it? Why were they here?"

Rev. Thomas stroked his chin. "Well, we are not far away from 'Watling Street,' which was an important road in roman times. Perhaps someone was travelling along it one day and lost the owl."

Rev. Thomas fumbled through his books for a few minutes. (He would find the Internet so much quicker, Toni decided.)

"Here we are!" Rev. Thomas announced, opening another book, his finger pointed along the route Watling Street had followed. Toni could see it went close to the village.

"The Roman probably stopped here to get some chips!" Toni laughed.

Rev Thomas was smiling too; Toni hoped he wasn't going to tell her the Romans didn't have chips in those days!

"What is the owl for though?" Toni asked.

"It's much the same as today really. Have you read any of the stories by Mr Milne? 'Winnie The Pooh,' I think they are called."

Toni nodded, "I have read all of those. There is an owl in those stories too. Pooh goes to ask the wise old owl questions."

"That's right! Athena was the goddess of wisdom and her symbol was an owl. People have thought owls are wise from ancient times."

"The one in Winnie the Pooh isn't very wise; he just pretends to be clever: he can't even write 'Happy Birthday' correctly."

"It's true, I had forgotten all about that. I was only reading that particular story to my nephew a few weeks ago!"

"HIPY PAPY BTHETHDTH THUTHDA BTHUTHDY" Rev Thomas tried to say.

Toni thought to herself, it was funny how books she liked in her own time, had been read by children a long time before she was even born. She decided not to tell Rev. Thomas the owl had made her friend Brenda's wish come true. Perhaps vicars did not believe in wishes and things like that.

"I had better be on my way," Toni stated, "Mrs Braithwaite will be wondering where I have got to."

Rev. Thomas thanked Toni for coming to see him.

"It made a nice change to talk to someone interested in Ancient Greece. You seem to know a lot about it. You must come again and read some of my books. I don't think they will be too hard for you."

"That is kind of you," Toni answered, "There aren't many interesting books in the village school: I would love to read one of your books."

Toni said goodbye and headed the short journey towards the Braithwaite's house. Her mother would have been shocked to hear she had been to see the village vicar. Mum and Dad never took her to church, but in this village it seemed to be something that everyone did on a Sunday morning

Chapter Nineteen
Good News / Bad News

It did not take Toni long to get back to the Braithwaites house. Edna had been wondering where she had been, until she remembered Toni telling her she was going to go to see Rev. Thomas after school, so she had not been worrying too long.

Tom had some good news and some bad news for Toni.

"Which do you want to have first?" he asked. There was a little smile in the corner of his face and a certain twinkle in his eye that could only mean the bad news wasn't so bad after all."

"I will go for the bad news first," Toni thought, "It is best to get it over with."

"I don't think you will be going to our village school tomorrow."

Toni was glum; she had begun to enjoy helping the younger children to read.

"What is the good news then?"

"Almund School is going to be open again."

"Oh!" she exclaimed, "I thought it was not going to happen for a long time, they said the school was in a dangerous condition."

"Apparently it is not quite as bad as they thought it was. The part of the school that has been damaged is going to stay closed, but they will be able to open another part of the school."

"It is going to be cramped in there with all the children in a small space."

"The letter we got this morning says the junior children will be going to school on Mondays, Wednesdays, and Fridays and the infant children on Tuesdays and Thursdays. I know it is not as much time in school as you get here, but it is a lot better than some children have. I have heard in London a lot of the schools have to stay permanently closed until after the war. The authorities think it is too dangerous for children to be in the city while there is bombing going on."

Toni was feeling much happier now; she quite liked Almund School and had good reasons for wanting to go back there again. Maybe she could find the book that had sent her back in time!

"What time does the Bus for Tuther leave in the morning?" She asked.

"There is only one bus a day, it leaves at six in the morning and then only comes back in this direction at six in the evening."

"It means I will have to hang around in Tuther waiting for the bus to bring me back here. I could be leaving here in the dark and then coming back in the darkness too.

"You could just stay in Tuther?"

"I don't think it would be fair to ask PC Gregg and his wife to let me stay there, they have enough to do already!"

Toni was beginning to think her hopes had been dashed. The war was having a terrible effect on the lives of people all over the country.

Tom led her out into the back yard.

"Edna and me don't want you to go back to living in Tuther. Not until all this bombing stops anyway, so we thought of something which might help you out a little. It is only three miles from here to Tuther so we thought perhaps you did not need to go by bus.

"You want me to walk three miles there and back every day?" Toni was surprised.

"No, we thought you could go on this!" Tom pulled an old oily sheet off an ancient bicycle. "I have been trying to fit it up for you so you can ride to school each day. The brakes work fine and the tyres have been pumped up so they are rock hard."

Toni stared at the bike. It was like something she had once seen in a museum. The brakes were worked by levers. She could see the rods going down to the wheels but there was no sign of any gears! Tom had painted the wheel rims black with some paint that he had found, to cover up any rust that was there. The rest of the bike was bright red, but Toni could tell it wasn't its original colour. There were wire springs under the seat that creaked when she pressed down on it.

Toni thought about the bike she had at home. It had sixteen gears on it and cable brakes. It was bright pink with gold flashes on the side. It even had pink streamers on the end of the handle bars. She had got it for her birthday, months ago, but it stayed in the shed most of the time.

Mum thought it was far too dangerous for her to ride her bike on the roads. A thundering great lorry or speeding car would be sure to knock her off and cause a serious accident. This meant she was only really ever allowed to ride her bike in the park, and then only if there was someone with her.

This seemed like a new exciting adventure for Toni. She had never been allowed to ride so far on her own before. Living in the 1940's did not have many good points, but this was certainly one of them. There was hardly any traffic on the roads. Not many people had cars of their own and of course there was a shortage of petrol and rationing.

"I hope you know how to ride a bike," Tom was saying, "I am sorry it is a boy's bike, the one Edna used to ride about on years ago went to the great scrap heap in the sky before the war!"

Toni felt she wasn't bothered about it being a boy's bike, but she hoped she could remember how to ride; it had been a long time and this heavy machine was very different from what she was used to.

"You never forget how to ride a bike!" Tom told her, "Though this one might be a bit too big for you. I have fastened some wooden blocks on to the pedals, so they should help."

It was only now Toni realised the bike was much bigger than the one she had at home. It was resting against the wall. Tom had lowered the saddle so it was as far down as it could go and he held on to it so Toni could get on. However, when Toni tried to sit on the saddle, her feet could not touch the floor. She was going to have a problem starting and stopping!

Together they pushed the bike out onto the road. They had to lean the bike against a wall so Toni could get settled. Tom offered to hold onto the saddle, but Toni thought she could manage. Once she was sitting on the bike, she pushed it away from the wall with her elbow and then started pedalling. The bike wobbled about for a few yards then Toni managed to get it going down the road.

It was a heavy beast, but with the slight incline of the road, she soon picked up speed and began to go quite quickly. Toni tried the brakes. There was a rumbling, grating sound as the worn down blocks tried to perform but they only managed to bring the bike slowly to a stop. There would be no emergency braking on this contraption!

Toni now took in the full horror of her situation. If she stopped, the bike would fall over, tumbling her into the road and the path of any oncoming vehicle. There was only one thing for it, she headed for a firm looking bush and ran into it. With the bike wedged into the bush she managed to fall off gracefully, without causing too much harm to herself or the bike. When she rode to school she would have to think of a different strategy –especially if there were no comfortable bushes around to crash into.

"I can run alongside holding out a mattress for you when you stop!" Tom suggested."Or you could tie pillows to yourself!"

Toni laughed.

Toni pulled the bike from the bush and turned it round to face back the way she had come. With the bike leaning on its side she placed a foot on a pedal and then pushed off from the floor with the other. The first time she tried it the bike wobbled and fell back onto the floor but Toni was not going to allow herself to be put off. The sight of old Tom running down the road to help her, spurred her on to try again. This time she got the bike upright after a few precarious, wobbly moments. With more practice, she would soon have the skill sorted although wearing a dress and trying to get her leg over the crossbar was another skill she had to master. 'Oh for a pair of jeans,' she thought!

The side of the Braithwaite's house had a long wall. Toni aimed the bike so she was travelling along the side of it slowly. Then she pulled the brakes on hard and came to a halt. By leaning in towards the wall she managed to stop without actually falling off. There was a scrape of whitewash on her shoulder, but it was easily brushed off.

Tom laughed loudly when he saw her rumble to a halt, but Toni didn't mind, she was determined to master this enormous beast one way or the other. Half an hour later, with one grazed knee and a scrape on her elbow, Toni pushed the bike back into the shed, satisfied she had nearly conquered her metal steed.

Chapter Twenty
Almund School

Toni could tell that Miss Booth was secretly quite pleased that she would not be going to Nuther Village School any more. The poor lady had far too many children in her class, though she was very grateful Toni volunteered to come in and help with reading, if she managed to get back from Tuther in time.

Edna had found an old canvas bag Tom had used before the war when he went out fishing. Toni thought it would be excellent for carrying her school books and an apple for lunch. Normally Toni would have not been seen dead with an ancient object like that round her shoulder, but she knew in war time England there were no stylish sports bags to be had. She just had to make do and put up with it. Miranda would have had hysterics, being seen without her 'designer' gear.

Toni decided to leave her Owl necklace behind. Miss Booth had commented a few times about not liking to see children wearing jewellery. She was sure the teachers in Almund School would not like it either. They would probably insist upon confiscating it, so Toni wrapped the necklace in its leather chord and placed it in her safe place, under the loose floor board in her bedroom.

The journey to Tuther was not long, but there were a few junctions where she would have to be careful and go in the right direction.

"I will follow all the sign posts to Tuther," Toni explained, "I won't get lost that way."

Tom shook his head, "There are no sign posts Toni, they were all taken down ages ago!"

"What did they go and do that for?"

"In case the Germans invaded, or a pilot from one of their shot down planes tried to find his way back to the coast."

"I must have forgotten about that," Toni corrected herself, trying to sound convincing, "I will need a small map on a piece of paper, in case I forget which way to turn."

Tom agreed to draw her one, but warned she must make sure she did not leave it lying around.

"It could fall into enemy hands!"

Toni wanted to laugh, but she could see that Tom was being serious.

"If I am captured by the Germans I promise that I will eat it rather than let them get it!"

Tom couldn't stop laughing.

Toni's Journey to school was quite uneventful, though she worried all the time about what she would do if she suddenly had to stop. The road junctions where she had to turn left and right did not present any problems; there was no traffic coming in either direction so Toni just slowed down before making her turns. Back home she would have been in serious trouble. She recognised the first junction as being one with traffic lights and the next one would be a roundabout in her time, with an entrance and exit to the new motorway. But in the 1940's these things had yet to be built.

Toni called in at the Gregg's house on her way, to see if her friend Lizzy was going to school too. Lizzy was jealous of Toni's bike and wanted to ride on the handle bars with her to school. Her policeman father put his foot down over that request.

"I have enough accidents and trouble to deal with while all this bombing is going on. I don't want to have to be carrying you off to hospital as well,"

He suggested Toni left her bike at his house, so the girls could both walk to school together.

"There aren't many bikes around these days," he told her, "petrol rationing has meant people cannot get around like they used to, so there have been a lot of thefts of bikes recently. If you leave yours unattended in the school playground, it will only be an invitation for someone to come along and steal it"

Toni and Lizzy set off for school together, wondering what the school would be like now.

The last time Toni had seen it, half the school's wall had been lying in a heap of rubble in the playground. As Toni and Lizzy walked along the road together, Toni noticed her friend turned left instead of right at the road junction.

"You are going the wrong way," Toni called, "School is that way!"

Lizzy laughed, "Didn't anyone tell you? School isn't there anymore. It has been moved. We are now in the Parish Church Hall." Toni was surprised.

"There were going to use part of the school that hadn't been damaged, but the roof fell down in one of the classrooms, so the idea was abandoned. Didn't you know?"

Toni told her the Braithwaite's didn't often have a local newspaper delivered, so they didn't know about anything going on in Tuther. It had only been through a friend that they had actually seen her picture in the paper.

Miss Atkin was waiting at the door of the Parish Hall as all the children began arriving for school. She was wearing a dark blue dress and the very high heels she wore made her look an imposing figure.

She went down her list and ticked their names off as they arrived.

"You must be Toni Braithwaite. I read all about you in the local paper. It mentioned that you were in our shelter when the bomb dropped. I don't know how you came to be in school that day; we don't have you down in any of our records! It is just as if you appeared here from nowhere!"

"I am sorry Miss," Toni tried to explain; "I don't know anything about the bomb or this school! The doctor had hoped my memory would come back soon, but I am sorry I am still not able to remember anything that happened or where I was living. It is all a total blank." Toni hoped that she would sound convincing, but the look on Miss Atkin's face warned she would have to be careful.

"I think she is a spy Miss!" Lizzy whispered, "The Germans dropped her by parachute into the middle of the town in the dead of night!"

Toni smiled at her friend curiously.

"She has been spying on us all the time; you can tell from her funny accent that she is not from here - and she loves sausages too!"

Toni was starting to get worried, and then Lizzy started laughing.

"Vot are you talking about, mien liebchen?" Toni said, in her best German accent.

"Really Lizzy, I am glad you are getting back to school, you have obviously been reading far too many of those dreadful comic books!"

The two girls walked into the Parish Hall, wondering what they would see in there.

Chapter Twenty One
Tuther Parish Hall

The parish hall was an immense rectangular room, with a high ceiling. There were thin iron beams running across the room from side to side, with large white lights hanging from them.

Organisation had been done at great speed, with Miss Atkin taking charge. Desks had been taken from the damaged school and were arranged in rows facing the door. There were a few blackboards lying around the room and piles of books and paper left where they had been dumped. It had obviously all been done very quickly.

There was an older man in some kind of army uniform standing by the door. He had a grim expression on his face and it seemed he was unhappy with the fact the children were to be in the church hall.

Miss Atkins followed the last of the children into the hall, only to be confronted by the man in uniform.

"This is most irregular Miss Atkin; I was not informed through the correct channels that you are taking over my premises!"

With the benefit of her heels, Miss Atkin raised herself to her full height and stared him straight in the eyes.

"This is not your building Mr. Carpenter: it belongs to the parish."

"Captain Carpenter if you please! It has been commandeered for the use of the Local Defence Volunteers, for the training of men from the community to defend our town from invasion by the Germans, I am sure even you can see how important it is!"

"**Mr Carpenter**, the room will be returned to you for your use at 4 o'clock or, if you prefer, 1600 hours. Until then I suggest you get back to your Estate Agents office and leave the vital education of our children to me!"

Toni smiled; there was obviously some friction between the two.

"I think they must really fancy each other!" Toni dared to whisper to Lizzy.

"Come along children," Miss Atkins called, "Please come and sit on the floor so I can talk to you all." Her voice echoed in the large room, along with the clatter of her shoes.

Captain Carpenter was affronted, "The LDV command will take a dim view of this, Miss Atkin!"

"LDV!" one of the boys shouted out, "It stands for: Look Duck and Vanish! Fat lot of good you old men will be if the Gerry's do land!"

There was laughter all round the room. Toni could see Miss Atkin was desperately trying to stifle her amusement.

"I hope you will seriously admonish that unruly child, Miss Atkin!" Captain Carpenter had gone bright red in anger and was beginning to spit as he shouted.

"Leave your grandson for me to deal with, Mr Carpenter! Now, if you please, can we get on?"

Toni and Lizzy settled down on the rough floorboards, waiting for Miss Atkin to speak.

"Good Morning Children, may I begin by welcoming you to our school. I know it is not the building you are used to, but it is children who make a school, not bricks and mortar."

Everyone was listening to her.

"As you no doubt heard, we have to share this building with the Local Defence Volunteers. They will expect to find this building ready for their use at the end of our school day, so it is up to us to make sure we make as little nuisance of ourselves as is possible.

The floor will have to be cleared of desks and tables, so when the men arrive, they will struggle to realise we have been here. For that reason, I urge you all to try and make yourselves as useful and helpful as you possibly can."

For the next half hour Miss Atkin divided the children up into teams. Each team was given a specific task. Some had to move desks away to be stored at the far end of the room; others had to move blackboards and tables into their correct positions. At first it seemed like total chaos, but with Miss Atkin's enthusiasm, everyone was soon working together to achieve the end result.

Toni didn't think moving tables and desks around had much to do with her education, but she enjoyed doing something useful, rather than sitting in Miss Booth's cramped classroom. It wasn't long before the children could move all their desks into position in less than ten minutes. All Miss Atkin had to do was to clap her hands twice and shout 'assemble' and they set to work like a well-oiled machine.

"This is a much better way to be doing our tables!" Toni told Lizzy.

The rest of the morning was spent organising the children into learning groups. Miss Atkin had two other teachers with her and a number of mothers who had been dragooned in to help. Toni managed to sit next to Lizzy on the front row, but Miss Akin threatened if they spent all their time talking instead of working, then they would both have to sit next to boys.

There weren't enough sum books to go round, so Miss Atkin wrote a lot of the lesson on her black board. Toni was amazed at how neat and straight Miss Atkin's writing was. She was easily able to reach to top of the board, which would have been beyond the reach of most of the other women.

Toni found the sound of the chalk scraping on the board made her feel queasy and when the board was cleaned off for the next lesson, the chalk dust made her cough and splutter but these things didn't seem to bother the others.

'It's another thing I'm going to have to get used to.' She mused to herself.

While Miss Atkin was teaching Toni's class, a different teacher was busy with some younger children at the other end of the hall. Toni found it quite distracting, especially when she was trying to read quietly. The other class seemed to spend most of their time chanting multiplication tables or singing songs. Mr Cuthbert would never have put up with that, but with over a hundred children of different ages in the room, silence was never going to be achieved for long.

The Parish Hall had a few smaller rooms leading off the main hall. One of these was being used by the Local Defence

Volunteers as their office, so it was firmly locked. There was, however, a small kitchen where tea could be brewed, but the lack of anywhere to play, both inside or out, was very upsetting.

"Time for a break!" announced Miss Atkin. "Everyone can go outside!"

To Toni's surprise, Miss Atkin had the street outside blocked off. Long skipping ropes had been tied to the railings on either side, so the children could play in the street for a while. No cars or buses came down the street, so playtime was quite safe for the children. The houses on the other side of the road had windows which were in great danger of being broken, so Miss Atkin had to ban the children from playing football or any ball games which might cause damage, but no-one seemed to mind - at least they were out in the fresh air!

Lizzy had brought a bag of marbles to school; she gave some to Toni so they could both play in the gutter. Toni wondered what her own mother would have thought, if she could have seen her daughter on her hands and knees, playing in the centre of a street like some kind of unruly urchin.

At lunchtime they both hurried home to Mrs Gregg's house, where Lizzy's mum made them something to eat. Some of the children went to 'British Restaurants' where they could get a plate of stew, but Lizzy didn't fancy eating her dinner standing up in a crowded room.

Back at school in the afternoon, an old piano, that had almost certainly never been tuned, was pushed out into the room. Miss Atkin played with great gusto, hammering out tunes on the poor instrument and leading the singing with her own high pitched, warbling voice. There were no song books, but most of the children seemed to know the words already. Toni found she was able to join in reasonably well, as they were singing some of the songs she had been learning in her 'Historical project.' It seemed 'Roll Out The Barrel' was a great favourite with all of the class, much to Toni's own disgust – she had never liked that one!

At the end of the school day, they had all the desks put neatly away and were ready to leave just as Captain Carpenter came storming into the hall. He was expecting to find his precious hall ruined but he stopped dead in his tracks when he realised Miss Atkin had been as good as her word. The room was exactly as she had promised it would be.

"Very good Miss Atkin, very good indeed! I hope this arrangement will continue in a like manner!"

"Are you going to apologise for your disgusting behaviour this morning, Mr Carpenter?" She asked, facing him eye to eye again.

"Apologise? Apologise, when you address me correctly and I may be inclined to give it due consideration!"

"Very good, Mr Carpenter, very good indeed: as long as we both know where we stand!"

Chapter Twenty Two
Americans

Lizzy and Toni walked home to the Gregg's house together. When they got there, Mrs Gregg had a visitor waiting to talk to Toni. It was Miss Goldburn from the library. She wanted to find out if Toni would be able to come and recite some poetry for her ladies the following day. Toni explained she would have to ride in from Nuther on her bike but did not think it would be a problem, since school for her age group was only on alternate days.

"I do hope you will be able to come along dear." Miss Goldburn explained, "Our ladies are perhaps the best cake makers in the town. They wondered if you would be able to help by judging our 'cake of the month' competition?"

"You want me to come along and eat cake!" Toni smiled, "I will be there, you can absolutely bet on that!"

PC Gregg was home when Toni and Lizzy arrived back from school, so he helped Toni set off on her journey back to Nuther by holding the bike steady for her. Toni risked taking one hand off the handlebars to wave good bye to her friend as she began to pedal away into the distance.

The road was just as quiet as it had been in the morning. She cycled past a farm cart loaded with hay, which was being pulled along by a large black horse. The driver was slumped to one side, fast asleep. Toni hoped his horse knew the way home.

She also saw the postman on his bright red bike, pedalling in the other direction. He raised a hand to wave, wobbled and then was gone.

It was all very different from the roads around her home, where heavy lorries and vans would sweep any cyclist into the side with the thorny bushes.

Travelling back the way she had come almost got her lost at a junction, but a thatched cottage on the corner reminded her which way she had to go.

It wasn't long before she had left the comparatively 'busy' Tuther behind and was heading out into the empty countryside. Fields lined both sides of the road, some with crops growing, some with cows wandering towards the farm house in time for milking. In one field she could see a lonely ploughman with his horse cutting neat furrows into the soil. A small flock of birds followed his path, no doubt eager to grab at any worms or insects the plough had turned up.

Suddenly her handlebars started to wobble about and the front wheel made a loud grating, grinding noise. Toni stopped abruptly and managed to roll onto the hard road. She got up, bruised and a bit shaken, and stood the bike against a hedge to see what the matter was. The front tyre was flat. It had punctured! She would now have to push the bike all the way back to Nuther.

The road was empty; there were no farm houses where she could go to for help, so she would just have to walk. The bike had seemed to be such an excellent idea. It had only taken her about half an hour to cycle to school that morning and now she was going to have to trudge the long way home. Her wounded, 'trusty steed' creaked painfully as she began to push.

Toni did not know how far she had to go, there were no milestones to help her, but she guessed she was just over halfway back to the Braithwaite's house. She hoped Tom had a puncture repair outfit somewhere, or it was going to be a long walk to Tuther in the morning.

Just as Toni was beginning to get used to pushing the bike along the road, she heard a loud rumbling coming from behind, then a large army truck went past. It pulled up a few yards in front of her and two men climbed down out of the back.

They were dressed in uniform, but they did not look like any of the uniforms of soldiers she had seen around Tuther.
"Hi there, little darling," An unusual voice called to her; "You got a flat there?"
Toni's Mum had told her she must never ever speak to strangers. This was something that had been drummed into her from her youngest age. Teachers at school were constantly telling them to be careful to be aware of 'stranger danger!' Yet here she was, on a lonely country road, miles from anywhere and anyone, with two total strangers walking towards her!

Toni noticed the badge on the side of the soldier's uniform and the large star on the side of their wagon. It could only mean one thing, they were Americans. Should she run away from men who had come over to England to help with the war against the Germans?

Toni decided the friendly smiles that approached her were not to be feared. These men were friends, whatever her mother and teachers at home might try to tell her.

"My tyre is flat." Toni sighed, thinking they might be able to help.

"You got a repair kit girl?"

"No, I am sorry I don't."

One of the men picked up the bike and began to carry it towards the truck.

"Where are you going with my bike?" Toni asked, feeling uneasy.

"I don't suppose a sweet young English Rose would mind accepting a lift from the army of the United States?"

He took her hand and soon Toni, along with her bike, were both carefully stowed in the back of the lorry.

The lorry had two long benches down both sides, on which more men were sitting. There was a think canvas cover which went over the top, making the inside quite dark. The men all budged up a little so they could make room for Toni.

"Where are you heading darling?" Toni was asked.

"I am going to Nuther Village, if you please." Toni answered.

"Will you listen to the voice of this one; she sounds like a regular princess! So polite and well-mannered too."

Toni laughed, not only at what the men were saying, but also at their strange accents. It was like listening to famous actors in a film.

"Would you like some gum child?" A friendly voice asked.

Toni looked round unsure what to say.

"Listen guys, this is a real English Princess we have here! We should introduce ourselves; you all know what it says in our book about the British we got. We have to have proper manners! I am Bret; this is Dave, Mike, Harry.... and Chuck!"

After they had all said 'howdy'. Toni began to feel better.

"What are you doing, way out in the country?" They asked.

"My house was bombed, so I have come to live with some relations of mine in Nuther, but I still go to school in Tuther."

"Did you hear that? This little lady has had her house blown up by them Germans? Are your Mom and Pop alright?"

Toni felt a lump in her throat; it was often there when someone asked her about her parents, "I don't know," she answered, "the explosion has made me forget everything."

The men seemed to be deeply moved, they hadn't been in England long and the reality of the war was only just beginning to come home to them. They didn't know what to say, but they opened up their bags and soon had Toni's pockets filled with all the chocolate and chewing gum they had. 'Juicy Fruit' was written on the side of the packet and Toni was sure she had seen that in shops before at home.

It did not take long for the truck to reach Nuther. Tom could not believe his eyes when he saw Toni climbing down from the back of the vehicle, followed by at least a dozen or so American soldiers.

"I got a puncture," Toni told him by way of an explanation, "and these kind men offered me a lift home."

Tom went and shook the hands of each of the Americans, one by one.

"You must all come in!" he implored, "I think Edna has a cake fresh out of the oven!"

The Americans eyed each other, wondering what they should do. An officer climbed down from the cab at the front.

"It's kind of you sir, but we have to get to our base before nightfall."

Edna had heard what was going on from her kitchen and came out, still wearing her apron, carrying the cake she had made.

"Then take this back to base with you," She begged, "I am sure it will go down well with all the coffee you all drink!"

The men got back into the lorry and then set off on their way. Toni watched as hands waved to her from under the canvas that was covering the truck.

Chapter Twenty Three
At the Library

Toni didn't know what to do about her bike. She didn't want to disappoint the ladies at the library and the thought of tasting all those different cakes was an opportunity far too good to miss. When Tom came home from work, he was happy to sort the bike out.

It would have been an easy job for Tom to fix the puncture on Toni's bike; he had done it many times before, but he decided it would be better if Toni did it herself.

"You might get another puncture on the way to Tuther, and then you would have to walk all the way there and back pushing the bike."

Toni tried to say something, but Tom was insistent, "You were lucky to be rescued by some American soldiers. They won't be there every time you know!"

Toni had to agree, it wasn't every day someone from a Hollywood film set stepped in to help her.

Tom stood back, refusing to give any hands-on help, but talking Toni through the repair process.

"You are lucky it is just the front wheel, the back one has the chain attached so it is much harder to do."

Toni struggled to turn the bike upside down. Her hands hurt as she tried to slacken the nuts holding the wheel in place, but with a few grunts and complaints she finally managed it and lifted the wheel clear.

Edna found two old serving spoons that would make excellent tyre levers. Tom showed Toni how to gently prise the tyre off, taking care not to nip the inner tube and cause more damage.

"If I get a puncture out in the middle of nowhere, how am I supposed to find two serving spoons?" Toni asked.

"There is a war on, young lady; you will just have to improvise!"

They carried the inner tube inside. Toni thought it was just like a long black snake, so she chased Maureen and young Tom round the kitchen with it.

Toni fixed the bicycle pump to the tube and inflated it a little. Tom showed her how to immerse it in the kitchen sink and look for the tell tale bubbles of air, which would show her where the puncture was. Young Tom was fascinated with what they were doing and had to be lifted up so he could sit on the edge of the sink and watch.

It took a while but eventually Toni could see a steady stream of bubbles coming from a tiny hole in the tube.

Tom had a puncture repair outfit; he showed Toni how to stick a black plaster over the hole with some special glue.

"You will be wanting me to kiss it better next" Toni laughed, the holding tube out so the two 'men' could examine it.

"Before you put it back inside the tyre, you should see if you can find out what it was that caused the puncture in the first place. If you just put it straight back in, it will only get another one."

Toni gently ran her finger round the inside of the tyre. It wasn't long before she felt something hard and sharp. Toni carefully pulled a thorn out of the tyre.

"I wouldn't have thought something as small as this could have caused so much trouble." She stated.

"Keep checking," Tom suggested, "You might find more than one thorn in there." Sure enough Toni found two more thorns, one of them much bigger than the others. With the wheel finally back in place, Tom helped Toni to wheel the bike back out onto the road.

"Now we will see how good you are at repairing a puncture!" Tom announced.

Toni began to get ready to ride the bike.

"My sister thought she had made a good job of it once, but when she got half way down our street the front wheel came off and she landed up in a prickly bush, so take care, Toni!"

Toni felt nervous, but the wheel seemed to be fine, even when she pulled the brake levers to see if it would still stop. Repairing the bike must have done something to improve the brakes because they now made the bike stop instantly. If she hadn't been careful, poor Toni would have been straight over the handlebars.

Tom found a small wooden box in his shed - he seemed to have one of everything in there. He fitted it behind Toni's saddle so there would be somewhere to store the repair outfit should it ever be needed. The box was also big enough for her to put the serving spoons in and a few of the things she might need for her visit to Tuther.

The journey to Tuther next day was easy. Toni now knew the route well and only stopped at one of the junctions to check which way she had to turn. Miss Goldburn was by the door waiting for her to arrive and helped her to bring her bicycle round to the back of the library, where it would be safe.

"There may be a war on!" Miss Goldburn explained, "but there are some people around who are almost as bad as Mr. Hitler. "You mustn't leave anything lying around or it may go missing."

There were about twenty or more ladies waiting inside the library. A large table which normally held copies of the newspapers had been cleared and laid with a crisp white cloth. Toni's eyes bulged wide as she saw all the cakes set out on it. They all looked mouth-wateringly delicious. Miss Goldburn introduced Toni to the ladies, explaining how Toni had become a local hero after what she had done to save all the children from the bomb at Almund School. Heads nodded all round the room. The ladies were obviously delighted to see someone so interesting.

Toni opened her book and carefully began to read the poem about 'Gus, the theatre cat.'

"*Gus is the cat at the theatre door*
His name, as I ought to have told you before"

Something strange happened. Toni was concentrating so hard upon the words of the poem. She could hear the music somewhere in her mind like before. The music helped her to keep the rhythm of the poem perfect, her expression exact. Toni suddenly realised she was not reciting the poem, she was singing it!

*"Is really Asparagus, but that's such a fuss to pronounce
That we usually call him just Gus!"*

Toni couldn't stop now, she had all eyes upon her, everyone was listening, and she had to carry on singing, her voice soft and clear. Toni continued and finally came to the last verse.

*And I think that I still can much better than most
Produce blood curdling noises to bring on the ghost
And I once played Growltiger.*

Her voice became softer

Could do it again

And quieter

Could do it again,

Until she could hardly be heard

Could do it again.

The ladies leapt to their feet and clapped loudly.

"My dear child, "Miss Goldburn said, "I have never heard anything so beautiful."

"I never knew the poem had music to it! I thought it was just ordinary!"

Toni grinned. She loved the comments the ladies were making and it made her feel shivery all over.

"Now, before we ask Toni to recite another poem, I think we should ask her to be the judge of our monthly cake making competition." Miss Goldburn asked.

"Please be kind dear," an old lady explained, "we can't get the eggs and sugar we used to have, so our cakes are nowhere near as good as they were before the war."

Toni knew she was going to enjoy this. Tasting cakes was her speciality! She took great care, cutting just a tiny slice from each cake. After tasting each cake, she had a sip of water so the taste of the previous cake did not clash with the new one.

There were twenty cakes to judge. Some had been decorated, others were just plain. Some had cream fillings, others jam, but the one Toni went back to was marbled with different colours and flavours. It was an easy decision to make, but Toni went back and tried just a little more of each cake before she made her final decision.

"Thank you," Toni announced, realising they were hanging on every word she spoke. "This has been a hard task," She could remember what the head teacher at her school said when he had to judge a competition.

"I am sorry I was not able to judge any of your cakes before the war, because if these cakes are anything to go by, then they must have been truly amazing. I know it is difficult to get all the things you need to bake a cake but you have all made perfectly delicious efforts."

The ladies all clapped their thanks again.

"But Miss Goldburn has asked me to choose a winner so after a lot of thought I have decided the one that is best is....."

Toni waited a few seconds, just like she had seen them do on television,

"This one!" Toni held up the marbled cake. The ladies all clapped again.

"I loved all the different flavours in this one Toni explained, it was absolutely scrummy!"

A lady called Evelyn who was sat at the back came forward blushing. Toni shook her by the hand and gave her a kiss on the cheek.

"Can we please hear another of those delightful poems?" Miss Goldburn asked.

Toni had her copy of Old Possum's Book of Practical Cat open. Her eyes were drawn to the first page of the book. There was something there she recognised. It meant the book was a first edition! In her time a book like this, in mint, perfect condition, would be worth an absolute fortune.

Toni opened the book at 'The Gumbie Cat' and began to sing.

> *I have a Gumbie cat in mind*
> *Her name is Jennyanydots*
> *Her coat is of the tabby kind*
> *With tiger stripes and leopard spots*

This time Toni got so carried away with the music which she could hear in her mind, by the time she came to the end of the poem she found she had been singing and dancing to the music.

The ladies all loved Toni's singing. It had been a long time since they had enjoyed an afternoon tea quite so much. Toni wanted to stay and recite and sing some more poems for her new friends but she knew it was a long way back to Nuther and it may start to get dark before she got home if she did not set off soon.

Reluctantly Toni climbed onto her bike and set off, the box at the back of her bike packed to bursting with quite a few extra slices of the delicious cakes the ladies had been making.

Chapter Twenty Four
Tom

Toni cycled carefully all the way back to Nuther. She tried to keep the bike away from the edge of the roads so there was less chance of running over a thorn again. There were no other cars or lorries on the road. The only person she saw was her lonely postman, cycling in the other direction; they both waved a hand as they passed on the empty country road.

As soon as she got to the Braithwaite's house Toni wheeled the bike round to the back and leaned it against the shed. The door to the kitchen was not locked; Edna had told her she never locked it, even at night. Toni suspected they had probably lost the key long ago.

There was a note propped up on the kitchen table Edna had left for Toni. She wrote she had taken Maureen and young Tom to visit a farm on the other side of the village. She had just heard their cow was having difficulty giving birth to a calf. Edna was good with cattle; local farmers often turned to her rather than call in an expensive vet from the town.

The kettle was boiling, as always, so Toni made herself a cup of tea and carried it through to the other room. She was startled to find Tom sitting in a chair, slumped over to one side. He did not look at all well.

"Are you alright Tom?" she asked.

"When I was working on the farm, I had this funny feeling, right in the middle of my chest." He told her, "It keeps coming and going all the time, I told old Mr Groves. He thought I didn't look too good, so he told me to go home."

"So you came back, straight away, that was good." Toni said.

"No, I thought the girls would think I was trying to get out of doing any of the work, so I went back to the barn. Then, when I was trying to lift a bale of hay, I had this pain all the way down my arm."

Toni rubbed Tom's arm where he said it hurt, but the pain seemed to keep moving. Tom rubbed his face saying he didn't understand it, his jaw was hurting now.

Toni did not know what she should do. Tom was finding it difficult to breath.

"You stay there! "Toni shouted, "I am going to get the doctor!"

Tom could hardly speak, "It's no use, it will be dark soon, and he lives at the other side of the village."

"Don't be silly, I have the bike, I will be there and back before you realise I have even gone."

Tom began to get up, he was pale, he seemed to be about to say something, but the words never left his mouth.

He tumbled forward and collapsed beside a chair, only missing the edge of a table by inches. Toni froze with fear; Tom was lying at her feet. He was unconscious and had stopped breathing; there was obviously something dreadfully wrong with him.

It was as if Toni was being controlled by some kind of automatic pilot. She knew exactly what she had to do. The word of her swimming teacher came back to her.

"If the casualty is not breathing you may have to help them to breathe. Remember ABC!"

Toni remembered A stood for Airway. She undid the top few buttons of Tom's shirt and made sure nothing was stopping him from breathing. Thankfully he was already on his back, so she tilted his head back just as she had been shown with the dummy on the side of the swimming pool.

Tom was still not breathing. B stood for breathing; she would have to breathe for him. Normally Toni would have run away quickly rather than attempt what she did next, but she tried to stay calm. She pinched Tom's nose closed and then put her own lips round Tom's and gave him two deep breaths, blowing into his lungs slowly and carefully. Tom was still not moving.

C stood for circulation. She had to see if he had a pulse. At the swimming pool the teacher had shown them how to find each other's pulse by gently placing two fingers on the side of each other's neck. Matty in her class had been unable to find Poppy's pulse, so the teacher teased him, saying that she must be dead! They had all laughed when Poppy went, "Woo, I am a ghost!"

Toni felt for Tom's pulse but she couldn't find anything. She tried feeling his wrist too, but there was no pulse there either.

"If there is no pulse you have to start doing compressions!" the teacher had explained. He had shown them how to find the casualty's sternum and then place their hands one on top of the other and began to push down firmly.

"Remember," The teacher said, "fifteen: two. Fifteen compressions followed by two breaths."

Toni counted to fifteen as she carefully pushed down on Tom. The teacher had told them they should now go and get an ambulance; they should dial 999 and get help. The Braithwaite's did not have a phone; she did not know where there was one in the village. So she did the only thing she could do; she carried on giving Tom compressions just as she had been shown, stopping every fifteen to give him two more breaths.

Toni carried on for what seemed like an age. Then, just as she was about to give up out of sheer exhaustion, she heard Edna and the children coming through the door.

Toni jumped up, "Quick Edna, take the bike, you have to run and get the doctor, Tom is ill, he needs the doctor now!"

Edna froze still, staring at her husband on the floor. Then she came to her senses and ran off to get the doctor. As she ran, Edna could be heard shouting to her neighbour to come and help look after the children, her shouts echoed round the village as she fled all the way to the doctor's house.

A neighbour, Mrs Alton, came in and quickly took little Tom and Maureen away to her own house. Another lady arrived to see if she could do anything to help. Just then Toni stopped pushing on Tom's chest and was about to give him another two breaths. She remembered she had to check Tom's pulse before she carried on. She carefully put two fingers flat against his neck. There was something there. It was very faint, hardly detectable, but it was there!

Something gurgled in Tom's throat: he sighed deeply and managed to take a breath on his own. Toni felt for his pulse again: it was stronger, much stronger than before. Tom's heart had started to beat again and he was breathing.

The neighbour moved forward, but Toni told her to go back, she knew exactly what she was doing. Taking great care not to bang or crack Tom's head on anything, Toni turned him onto his side into what she knew was called the 'recovery' position.
"I will make him some hot sweet tea then!" The neighbour announced.
"Oh please, no!" Toni insisted, "We must wait for the doctor to arrive."

There was a rumbling sound outside the house, followed by a loud screech of rusty brakes.
"He's here!"
Doctor Roberts rushed into the room clutching his black bag. He stared down at Toni with a look of incredulity written on his face.
"What is this child doing with Mr Braithwaite?"
"Thank you for getting here so quickly," Toni said, ignoring his query, "I think he has had some kind of heart attack. He slumped to the floor and stopped breathing, I tried but I couldn't find a pulse anywhere," Toni gave her report with a calm voice, "When I found his heart had stopped, I started CPR as I have been shown. I think I did it for about ten minutes, then when I checked his pulse it had come back and he was breathing again, so I put him into the recovery position."

Toni immediately stood up and moved out of the way so the doctor could examine Tom himself. Dr Roberts stayed on his hands and knees beside Tom for quite a few minutes. He had taken his stethoscope out and was listening to Tom's heart. Then he turned to look at Toni, his brow deeply furrowed in consideration.

"You say he collapsed onto the floor?"

Toni told the doctor what Tom had been saying before his collapse. When she mentioned the pain in Tom's arm and chest the doctor nodded.

"I am astounded beyond belief, young lady. You describe the symptoms of heart failure almost exactly. I have examined Mr Braithwaite most diligently and I can, without any compromise, confirm your diagnosis. He has indeed had severe heart failure and must be taken to hospital immediately."

"I was going to make him some hot sweet tea," The neighbour complained, "but this girl stopped me."

The doctor smiled at Toni again.

"I am glad you stopped her young lady! You seem to have some amazing medical knowledge for one so young!"

Quite a crowd had collected outside, so Dr. Roberts sent one of the men who was standing by the door to the vicarage, where he knew there was a telephone, telling him to be quick about making the call.

Tom was still lying in the recovery position where Toni had placed him. There was a gurgle in his throat and then his eyes opened. Tom rolled onto his back looking round the room. He was obviously confused.

"Welcome back, Mr Braithwaite." The doctor smiled, "It seems to me this young lady has just saved you from oblivion!"

Edna was on the floor next to her husband, holding his hand and gently stroking his brow.

Dr Roberts stood up and called Toni to him. He put a gentle hand on her shoulder.

"Tell me, Toni isn't it, what is this CPR you just mentioned?"

"I am not sure," Toni admitted, "My teacher used some long words I think it was something like cardio pulmer resuss ..." She stopped, getting the words all mixed up, "Well something like that."

Dr Roberts was stroking his chin, "I have never heard of anything like that. Cardio is a Latin word that means heart, 'pulmer' as you say is 'pulmonary,' which is to do with the lungs and that other word?"

"Resuss... resusishon?"

He laughed, "Resuscitation!"

"That's right!"

The doctor had Toni describe exactly what she had done; he even lifted up his own shirt so she could show him where she had placed her hands to push down on Tom.

"Words fail me Toni! I really do not understand any of this. You have obviously been taught what to do by someone who was experienced and had excellent medical knowledge. You don't know what you were doing or why you did it but I think it is safe to say you have just saved Mr Braithwaite's life!"

The doctor didn't have a chance to say any more. Tom was slowly coming round and was beginning to recognise where he was and smile weakly at Edna, his wife. The sound of the ambulance's bell ringing got everyone ready to help get Tom quickly into hospital."

Chapter Twenty Five
Tea

With Tom in hospital and Edna trying to get into Tuther as often as she could to see him, Toni was happy to help out by looking after young Tom and Maureen. The two children were difficult to babysit. Tom wanted to be out in the woods and fields doing something but Maureen preferred to be inside near the fire. One wanted to be drawing or painting or making something neat and tidy, whilst the other wanted to be running, climbing and coming as near to danger as any grownups would let him.

"I usually go to see my mother once a week. You could take Tom and Maureen there if you like - they love going to see Nanny Botley."

Toni had never heard any mention of Nanny Botley before. Her parents had never talked about that name. She seemed to be someone who had vanished into the distant past without leaving so much a ripple to say they had once existed.

Maureen held Toni's hand all the way to Nanny Botley's house. Tom ran ahead. He had found a stick and was playing his favourite game, diving between walls and bushes; shooting any Germans he found hiding.

Nanny Botley lived in a village called Wether. It wasn't far, but the children were soon complaining about the walk.

"My legs are heavy!" Maureen said, "You can carry me."

Toni shook her head, Maureen might be able to sit on her father's shoulders, but she was nowhere near as strong. The young children's strength soon returned when they saw the tiny trail of smoke rising from Nanny Botley's chimney.

Nanny Botley had a neat, tidy cottage, right next to an RAF airfield. It must have been some kind of pilot training place, because there was a constant stream of all sorts of aeroplanes flying in and out.

Nanny Botley had a huge garden into which the children immediately vanished without saying as much as a 'hello' and leaving the poor old lady standing at the door, wondering who had brought them.

Toni held out her hand, unsure of what she should do.

"Hello, I am Toni. I am sorry but they seem to be more interested in your garden."

"Oh so you are Toni! Nice to meet you dear, do come in and have some tea. They will be happy playing around with the animals."

Animals? Toni went up on her toes to look over the hedge. She could see two goats being chased by Tom. Maureen was carrying a broody hen. They both seemed to be perfectly at home.

"Tom will be alright until he decides to chase my Billy around, he won't stand for it."

Toni could see someone else in the garden. He was quite big compared to the other two.

"Who is that?" Toni asked pointing towards the other boy.

"Oh him, he's the dummy. He isn't right in the head. Should be put away if you ask me, but his stupid mother keeps him at home.

Toni was shocked. She had never heard someone talk about a handicapped person like that before.

There was a little cardboard sign propped up in a window by the front door. Toni read it as she followed Mirriam into the house.

'Beware of the Dog'

"You have a dog too!" Toni said excitedly, suddenly realising she had hardly seen a single dog since she had endured the terrible bomb.

Mirriam stopped still.

"Oh! You saw the sign. I didn't have the heart to take it down, after Benji had to go."

"Was he very sick?" Toni noticed a little tear in the corner of Mirriam's eye.

"The war dear, we have all had to make a lot of sacrifices, it has been very sad and difficult in lots of different ways." Mirriam turned to walk on into the house. Her voice made it obvious the subject was closed to further discussion.

Nanny Botley had shuffled off towards the kitchen and Toni followed, concerned she really should be keeping an eye on the children.

"Would you like a cup of tea Toni?" the old lady asked reaching for a kettle was bubbling away on the stove.

"Yes please Nanny." Toni answered.

"I don't think that I am *your* nanny dear, you can call me Aunty Miriam if you like."

Miriam; now there was a name she had heard before. There was a rolling pin in the drawer at home: Mum had told her it used to be old Miriam's.

Soon a cup of tea was handed towards her. Toni took care; she still was not used to cups with saucers. Any moment now, the cup was liable to go skating round and then shatter onto the floor.

Toni's face became distorted; she practically gagged! The taste of the tea was smacking her in the mouth like something putrid.

Miriam smiled,

"Tea made with goats milk takes a little getting used to dear. Would you like some honey in it? I haven't got any sugar."

"No, thank you," Toni said. She didn't think mixing the flavour of sickly honey was going to do anything to the flavour of this rancid tea.

Toni could hear shouts coming from outside, she wanted to go out and discover what was going on, but Miriam seemed to be oblivious to the noise.

"Give me your hand then dear," Miriam asked, "I always like to have a look at the palms of any new visitors."

Tom came running into the kitchen; he had something vitally important to tell his Nanny, but forgot what it was when he saw her holding Toni's hand. Tom brushed Toni's hand away.

"Read mine Nanny. Tell me what I am going to be!"

Miriam took hold of the child's hand and examined it carefully.

"When you grow up you are going to deliver coal!" she announced.

"A coal man?" Tom was disgruntled.

"Well that's all I can see, young Tom! Your hand is as black as the night!"

Tom ran off. He was more interested in his game.

"Now let me see your hand, Toni dear."

Toni held out her hand so the old lady could examine it.

"This is strange," Miriam pondered, taking off her thick glasses and cleaning them so she could see clearly, "Very strange indeed. You have got two life lines! "

Toni stared at her own palm and followed Miriam's finger as it traced the lines on her hand.

"Look this line starts here and then it just stops. That is odd. Then a line continues next to it."

One life stopping and then beginning again. Toni thought it was interesting.

"Does the first line start again?" Toni asked.

The old lady peered at her over the top of her glasses.

"Of course not, it would be impossible. You cannot hop backwards and forwards from one life to another!"

Miriam shook her head again, "It's no use, your hand is too confusing. I will have to try the tea leaves instead."

"Drink your tea Toni and we will see what the leaves say about you."

Toni grimaced. Miriam's tea was disgusting, but she took all of her courage in both hands and drank it, all in one go. She barely managed to prevent herself from being sick all over the floor.

Miriam took Toni's cup, turned it upside down in the saucer and then turned it round three times. A little of the dregs leaked out under the cup but Miriam didn't seem to be bothered.

"How do you read tea leaves?" Toni asked, "It sounds difficult,"

"It's not really hard, I have a booklet that tells me what it all means, I have been doing it for so long I don't usually need to look things up." Miriam reached behind her with one hand and fetched a well worn book from a shelf. She handed it to Toni.

"I start at the handle of the cup and then work round in a clockwise direction to look for pictures or symbols in the tea leaves."

Toni moved round so she could look over Miriam's shoulder; this sounded fascinating.

"Look! Do you see there? What do you think it is?" She was pointing with the sharp end of a finger nail.

"It looks like some kind of face."

"That's nearly right, it's a mask and it could mean you have a big secret you are hiding."

Toni went bright red.

"People wear a mask when they don't want others to know who they are."

"Oh, I see," Toni tried to make her stumbling voice sound normal but she was quickly realising there were some things she could not hide from Miriam.

"And there is a ball – it means 'travelling.' The ball is resting on a funny looking line: it seems to stop and begin again just like the life lines on your hand!"

"What does the line mean then?"

"It means a journey, but yours has been broken."

Toni tried not to look as if she understood; she didn't dare give anything away.

"A tree means a long life; this is funny - you have got two trees! That's two lives, it doesn't make any sense."

Oh yes it does! Toni thought to herself.

"There is a wheel there too; look those are the spokes of the wheel!"

Toni nodded, she could see it. Miriam was definitely not just making things up.

"A wheel means there has been something you had no control over, something you could not stop happening! And there is the reason - if I am not much mistaken, that is a bomb!"

She pointed towards a shape it looked clearly like a bomb; it was even complete with tail fins!

Miriam had finished looking at the tea leaves and stayed silent for a minute or two, mulling things over for herself. Toni waited, wondering how close to the truth the tea leaves would get. Would they show her eventually going home to her Mum?

"Something happened; I think it was a bomb. It has made one part of your life end and another begin. It is as if you have two separate lives. You started with one and then moved to a different one."

"Does it say I will go back to the other life? The one I had before the bomb?" Toni asked.

"I don't think so, that would be impossible wouldn't it? You can't change and then be unchanged, but there are some scissors there in the corner and I've no idea what they mean."

Toni looked at the tea leaves herself. Perhaps it wasn't a bomb after all - maybe it was the owl, hanging from a leather string round her neck.

Suddenly there was a loud noise coming from the garden: someone was crying and it sounded as if they were in pain.

Chapter Twenty Six
Godfrey

Toni rushed into the garden to see what was going on. Miriam didn't seem bothered, but Toni wanted to make sure Tom and Maureen were not hurt. She need not have worried: Tom and Maureen were not the ones in pain.

Tom was the child who was causing all of the trouble. He was standing in the middle of the garden, throwing stones at the boy Miriam had said was not right in the head. Godfrey, whom Toni recognised straight away as being someone who had Down's syndrome, was crying bitterly. Not all of Tom's stones had actually hit poor Godfrey, but enough had struck home to cause him a lot of discomfort.

"What are you doing?" Toni shouted rushing towards Tom and sweeping any remaining stones from his little hand.

"It's him, the dummy!" Tom shouted.

"Don't you dare call him that, leave him alone! What has he ever done to hurt you?"

"He keeps saying the plane that flew over was a Glouster Gladiator, but it was a Spitfire!"

Toni was exasperated, "that is absolutely no reason at all to go throwing stones at the poor boy!"

"But he doesn't know anything. He is wrong!"

Toni wished she could settle the matter but her knowledge of military aircraft was limited.

"There it goes again!" Tom shouted, watching the plane as it soared into the sky, "It's a Spitfire!"

Even a poor 'helpless girl' like Toni knew the difference between a plane with two wings and one with four!

"It is a Gladiator!" Godfrey was shouting and Toni spotted he was waving a much worn book in the air.

Toni decided to go over and settle the disagreement for herself. Godfrey was holding his copy of the 'Penguin book of Aircraft Recognition.' He handed it to Toni, his grubby thumb pointing to the right picture.

"Can I show this to Tom, please?" Toni asked. Godfrey nodded, his eyes following her every movement, worried in case his prized possession would be damaged.

Toni took the book over to Tom and showed him the picture in the book.

"He is right, Tom, it really was a Gladiator, not a Spitfire at all."

Tom sloped off to play his own game. He turned round suddenly and scowled in her direction.

"What do you know any way? You're a girl!"

Toni checked Maureen was ok. She was still stroking the soft feathers of a brooding hen, so Toni went back to talk to Miriam.

"Alf has just been!" Miriam announced, "He has left two rabbits for me!"

Toni eyed the furry creatures laid out on the draining board. They both had startled expression in their eyes.

They must have heard the bang before they were hit, Toni thought to herself.

"What are you going to do with them?" Toni asked.

Miriam had cleared the kitchen table and placed two large brown dishes on it.

"We" she explained with some assertion, "are going to make two rabbit pies!"

"They have still got their fur on!" Toni exclaimed.

"Then you will have to learn how to take it off. Bunny won't be doing it himself, will he?"

"I have never skinned a rabbit!"

"Well then, isn't it about time you learnt? There is a war on. Fresh meat is difficult to find, so a well-cooked rabbit is not only free, it's delicious."

Toni wasn't so sure; she didn't want to eat a bunny.

"But before we begin, I am going to need some flour, so if you will pop down the road to Mr Rogers our grocer, I will dig up and then peel all the vegetables."

Toni took Miriam's shopping basket and a pocket of food coupons before she headed for the shop.

*

There was no sign of Mr Rogers when Toni walked into the shop, but she could hear some loud groans and grunting coming from somewhere at the back.

Mr Rogers appeared, carrying a large box of biscuits.

"I hope you have coupons child! I have nothing off ration today!"

Toni explained that Miriam had sent her for some flour. Mr Rogers grunted again.

"You will have to wait while I attempt to carry a sack of flour in here!"

"You look as if you could do with some help in the shop Mr Rogers. You need someone to do all the carrying while you serve the customers."

"Chance would be a fine thing young lady! All the able bodied men have been called up to serve in the army, so there is just me."

An idea lit up inside Toni's mind.

"Hang on there a minute Mr Rogers; I think I know just the person who can help you out."

Toni ran all the way back to Miriam's garden where Godfrey was still standing, looking at all the planes flying overhead.

"Godfrey!" She called to him, "Would you like a job? A proper one?"

Godfrey nodded and followed Toni back to Mr Roger's shop.

"This is Godfrey, Mr Rogers." Toni announced leading her new friend into the shop.

"The dummy! He is useless! What good is he here?"

"That is cruel, Mr Rogers." Toni gave him a stern look that made the man wither, "Godfrey can read a bit, he's got his own book; and I am sure he knows the difference between a box of biscuits and a sack of flour! Look at him; he has bigger muscles than both of us!"

Mr Rogers didn't know what to say.

"Godfrey, could you go into the back room and fetch Mr Rogers here a big box of tea?"

"Ok, Godfrey will do it," he said, and to their surprise, he saluted and off he went.

"You just have to give him a little time and be patient with him; but he is strong and desperately wants to please everyone."

A few seconds later, Godfrey appeared, carrying a large packing case of tea. The case must have been heavy but Godfrey didn't seem to notice.

"Godfrey has got box!" he grinned, delighted with himself.

"I would never have thought it was possible, young lady, but I think you are right. Godfrey might not be able to do much but he can't half carry a box!"

"So you will give him a chance, Mr Rogers?"

"He can stay for the rest of the day, if he behaves himself and doesn't annoy my customers, he can have a job. "

"Oh thank you Mr Rogers, just give him time but most of all don't go shouting at him, he is easily upset."

By the time Toni's flour had been weighed out and wrapped in paper for her, a delivery lorry had arrived outside. Without being told, Godfrey went out and carried all the heavy sacks and boxes through to the store room.

Mr Rogers was delighted and called Godfrey over.

"If you are going to work here, you will need to wear an apron like a proper grocer." He carefully fastened and tied Godfrey's brown apron in place.

If he had won a trophy, Godfrey would never have been more pleased, Mr Rogers was happy too, the work was getting too heavy for him these days and customers hated to be kept waiting.

Toni went back to Miriam, to find she had kindly cut off the rabbit's feet and heads so she didn't have to do the gruesome part.

Miriam now showed her how to make a small cut and peel away the rabbit's skin. Toni thought it was grotesque but understood it had to be done.

Chapter Twenty Seven
A Challenge

Edna was already home by the time Toni arrived back with the children. She was standing in the kitchen wondering what she could prepare for their dinner when Toni placed a large wickerwork basket on the table. Edna lifted a cloth to reveal a freshly baked rabbit pie.

"Did Nanny Botley make this for us?" Edna asked.

"Not exactly," Toni answered, "I made the pastry and helped to cut up the meat and vegetables!"

"Clever girl! We will make a cook out of you yet."

Toni had something else to give Edna; on her way home past the grocer's shop, Mr Rogers had rushed out and given her a large jar of his own best marmalade. Toni told Edna about how she had got Godfrey a job in the shop.

"That's wonderful, there are a few boys like Godfrey around: I am sure they could all do something, rather than be locked up in a home. I am surprised he listened to what a little girl was saying though, he is usually very grumpy!"

"I told him off for saying Godfrey was a dummy. I think he knew it was the wrong thing to say nasty things about someone."

"You are right Toni, children like Godfrey always get picked on; their lives must be miserable."

During the night Toni woke up with a start. Something Nanny Miriam had been saying when she read her palm had made her begin to think. She had been happily living one life then a bomb had totally changed her world. It was as if the bomb had unlocked a door to the past. Maybe another bomb would let her go back to the future, where her mum was?

She could go to Tuther during an air raid and try to be near a bomb when it landed. Toni shuddered at the thought; it could also mean she would be blown to pieces!

Toni lay in bed wide awake, thinking things over. She was wrong; the bomb had not changed her life. She had already been in the past when the bomb exploded. She had been in the shelter with all the other children whose names were in the book. It was the book that had brought her here and the book might take her back, if only she could find it again.

Toni sat up in bed. She knew where the book was! It was inside Almund School, but the school had been badly damaged and was closed until it could be repaired. If Toni could get back inside the school then she could find that book! For the first time since that terrible bomb had exploded, Toni had some sort of plan to get herself back to her Mum.

The next day was a school day in Tuther, so Toni set off early. She had a plan in mind, to see if she could sneak inside the old school and find the one thing she needed, before she had to go to the church hall with the others.

Toni cycled as quickly as she could, going straight to Almund School. The last time she had been there, just after the bomb, there had been men stopping anyone from going near. Now there was just some barbed wire wrapped round the locked gate. There was a notice that said, 'Danger Keep Out.'

Toni cycled round the school, looking to see if there might be a different way to get inside. She saw there was a window at ground floor level, but Toni did not recognise where it was and could not decide where it would lead to, inside the school. The window was cracked, it would be easy to pull a broken piece of glass out and then find the lock that secured it. She could lean her bike against the wall and then stand up on it and climb in through the window.

It was a good plan, it would be easy to get inside but there was only one problem; the window was on a busy street. There were houses on the other side of the road. Someone would be bound to see her climbing in through the window. They would go to the wardens and then she would get caught and be in serious trouble. There had to be a better plan.

The wall to the playground was high with tall railings on the top. Toni had sometimes wondered if these railings were there to keep the unwanted out, or to keep the children in! The other side of the wall was in a quiet lane that ran down the backs of some old houses. One or two of them were already in a sad state of ruin and nearly all of the others had their windows boarded up. If she could climb into the playground from here, no one would see her.

Toni lent her bike against the wall and carefully climbed up onto the seat. She felt like a performer in a circus as she delicately balanced on one leg reaching up to touch the railings. All she needed to make the scene perfect was a couple of seals with colourful balls balanced on their noses.

Toni stretched up as high as she could, standing on her tip toes to reach the railings. If she succeeded, then she would be able to pull herself up onto the wall and over the railings into the playground. It would be easy once she was inside the big playground; she could find a way into the school and search for that book.

There was only one problem; it was just a tiny one: it was just 'two inches,' to be exact! That was the distance between the tip of her finger and the railings. Toni bent her knee a little and then sprang up from the bike's seat to grab hold of the railings.

She missed! She slid down the wall and collided with the bike, knocking it over. Toni was lying entangled in the pedals and crossbar of the bike, a stream of blood darkening her leg as it dripped from the deep cut in her knee. Toni rubbed her head to check there wasn't any other damage and decided to find something to stench the bleeding from her leg. She could come back later and try the plan out again. It might take a few attempts but Toni was sure it would eventually work.

Toni picked up her bike and began pushing it towards the Parish Church. Her leg hurt far too much to cycle just for now.

Chapter Twenty Eight
School

Toni pushed her bike around the corner, limping with each step she took.

"Goodness Toni!" A familiar voice sounded in her ears. "What have you been dong to yourself?"

Miss Atkin was staring down at her from her great, shoe-assisted height.

"I fell off my bike Miss," Toni explained, realising Miss Atkin was walking towards her.

"You are in the wrong place Toni, school is in the parish hall now!"

"I know Miss, " Toni stumbled to find something to say, "I was a bit early so I came over here to have a look at the school, I was wondering if anything had been done yet to repair it." She hoped her quickly thought up excuse sounded convincing enough.

Miss Atkin gave her a stern look, "That cut looks nasty!" she soothed, bending down to wrap a white handkerchief round Toni's knee. "Does it hurt a lot?"

"Not much Miss, it's one of the things you tend to get used to when you start riding a bike! Especially when it is too big for you!"

Miss Atkin was also carrying a bunch of keys.
"Since you are here and not too badly damaged you can give me a hand."
Toni wondered what her teacher wanted her to do now.

"I have been given special permission to get some books from the school. One of the wardens is going to come with me and make sure I do not go into any of the dangerous rooms."

Toni's eyes opened wide: she had never expected this.
"I want to collect some books for the younger children to read. You have no idea how difficult it is to teach reading when everything has to be written out over and over again on a black board. You can come in if you like and carry some books for me."
If I like! Toni thought, *I almost broke my neck trying to get in here!*

Warden Smith was waiting at the main entrance for them. If he had wanted to tell Toni to wait outside, he would have been wasting his time, Miss Atkin just brushed past him: this was her school and she would decide who was allowed to come in. Toni followed close behind. She was really going to be given a chance to find that book.

"Have you been the head teacher at the school for a long time Miss Atkin?" Toni asked, as they climbed the stairs together.
"Not really Toni, there was a Mr Rusham in charge before me, but he was called up to join the air force so the Local Education Board got me to step in. With all the men gone to war we had to take over."
"I don't suppose there were many ladies who were head teachers before the war Miss."
"That is quite right Toni; I was head teacher of a small village school before I came here. It was the only kind of school they let 'us females' have!"

"Will you have to go back to the village school when Mr Rusham comes back after the war then Miss?" Toni was full of questions today.
"Sadly that will not happen, poor Mr Rusham's plane was shot down over France; he did not survive. Anyway, interesting though your questions are, Toni, we have to get on. There are lots of books and papers we need to take to the Parish Hall."

Toni had found the special book lying on a table upstairs, in a place where it had been discarded. Surely this book had been more important in the past; someone had used it to record all the events in the school's history. There was only one place where it could be now and that was inside Miss Atkin's own office.

Miss Atkin could hear Warden Smith as he pounded up the stone steps behind her and Toni. Toni smiled to herself; one of them was wearing big heavy army boots, the other clattering along in slender polished shoes with exaggerated height: it was an interesting contrast in footwear!

The first classroom they went into was on the undamaged side of the school. If Warden Smith had thought he was there just to ensure safety, he was wrong! He was soon laden with a huge pile of books as copy after copy of 'essential texts' was loaded into his arms.

"Be a helpful young man and take these down stairs for me please!"
 Miss Atkin's' *please* seemed to have an echo of, '**Now!**' within it, so he reluctantly did as he was asked.

It wasn't long before Warden Smith was running up and down the stairs like Miss Atkin's own personal servant. Toni's task was merely to load him up again, each time he returned.

Miss Atkin attempted to move to a room on the other side of the building, but Warden Smith managed to stop her by blocking her path.

"The side of the room is missing," he asserted, "The whole wall has collapsed, and you cannot go in there."

It was his turn to be the one in authority now.

"I am not going in!" Miss Atkin assured him, "You are!"

With some reluctance, Warden Smith entered the room. Desks and tables still stood in the open air, facing the perils of wind and weather.

"What do you want me to bring?" he asked, his voice sounding unsteady, like the room around him.

"Oh really, if it is too much bother I will get young Toni here to help me. I only want to retrieve Miss Gorlick's bag from beside her chair! She has been worried about it."

With the speed of a sloth, Warden Smith made the precarious journey to the teacher's desk. He did not dare to look down towards the playground. It seemed to want to draw him into its deep, blackened jaws.

After half an hour Miss Atkin had recovered most of what she required from the school. There was only one more room Toni hoped she would visit: her office. Toni was not disappointed. Fortunately, Miss Atkin's office was on the safe side of the school and Toni walked into the office behind Miss Atkin, watching, whilst the head teacher busied herself collecting together important registers and papers.

There it was, lying closed on the edge of her desk.

"Do you want me to take this down?" Toni asked, nonchalantly, her hand smoothing over the leather cover of the book.

"Oh that, I suppose so; if you want to, though I really have not got time to be writing things in it just now."

Toni picked the book up and held it tight.

The two were soon back out onto the street, where they found the huge pile of books had been carried down for them by Warden Smith stacked at the doorway.

A sudden crash and a yell startled them both.

A little further down the street a young boy was lying on the pavement entangled in Toni's bike. Toni strangely recognised him.

"What is Billy Preston doing with my bike?"

"I know him!" Miss Atkin shouted running towards the wreck, "That's Frank Preston! I had to have him expelled last year!"

Frank was lying in a hopeless heap wailing mournfully clutching his leg through the bike's crossbar.

"Serves you right," Miss Atkin admonished, "You shouldn't take things that don't belong to you!"

"He was trying to steal my bike?" Toni exclaimed.

"Yes I think he was! But he didn't get very far did he? That Preston family have a lot to answer for. Perhaps one day they will learn."

Toni stared at the absolute image of Billy, "I don't think so Miss Atkin, I really don't!"

Toni picked up her bike. It was none the worse for its tumble, which was more than could be said for Frank. They left him where he was and returned to the school door.

"This is quite a collection, Miss Atkin. Shall I put a few on my bike and head off towards the Parish Hall?" Toni asked.

"Dear me no Toni, you have a bad cut that needs seeing to. I am sure under the circumstances, Warden Smith here will be only too willing to deliver the books, after all he does have the use of the warden's lorry at his disposal."

"Miss Atkin, the lorry is for the transportation of vital wartime supplies!"

"Very good, Warden Smith, I knew you would see it our way! Please knock loudly when you arrive; it is often difficult to hear anything with the whole school housed in just one large room."

Warden Smith tried to say something but he seemed to know that 'resistance was useless!'

Toni had the leather bound book she was interested in by her side. Miss Atkin had not noticed. She had her nose in the air, putting on the airs and graces of someone in authority, less Warden Smith should refuse and force her to do all the 'book carrying' by herself.

Whilst Miss Atkin had been instructing the Warden, Toni managed to slip the book into the box Tom had fastened to the rear of her bike, thanking heaven the adults were too busy to notice. She would have to wait until she was back with the

Braithwaite's before she could examine the book's contents carefully.

Chapter Twenty Nine
The Book

Toni had managed to keep the big book hidden away from the prying eyes of Miss Atkin for the entire day. Not wanting to leave it in the box on her bike in case it got stolen, she deftly and secretly transferred it to her bag and had it on the floor by her feet for the entire morning. Once she accidentally kicked it and it slipped out of her hiding place! She had needed to scrabble around on the floor to retrieve it before anyone noticed.

Twice Miss Atkin had commented, "Toni dear, don't you think your bag would be better off hung up on a peg?"

Toni had just smiled, getting on with her work, hoping their journey together into the damaged building might have forged a new bond between them. The book was quite heavy, nosey Miss Atkin would be sure to start asking questions.

"This looks interesting Toni, what have you brought in to show us today?" had to be avoided at all costs.

When the lorry load of books arrived at the hall, Miss Atkin made the men carry them inside and arrange them on shelves she had cleared. The children were delighted. It was good to have their old books back again; they were getting tired of having to copy everything down from the board.

After a fairly painful journey home, during which she stopped twice to adjust her constricting bandage, Toni finally felt safe, but it seemed ages before she could make an excuse to go up to her room and get a moment alone. At last she was sitting on her bed with the journal open on her lap.

The book was bound in leather with the title:

'Almund School'

Embossed in large letters on the cover. Inside the front page there was just a single sentence written in large letters.

'Turn the page to find out how we live."

The first page detailed the opening of the school in 1935 when the school was built to serve the growing town. On opening day April 1st there were 496 children on roll. The book also mentioned that besides the daily lessons, the school was used for evening classes in reading writing and mathematics for anyone in the community.

On 21st January 1936 reference was made of an announcement given at morning prayers that King George V had died.

In 1936 the town received its charter as a Borough from the new King Edward VIII and on 22nd December 1936, the Mayor visited the school to present commemorative medals to the children.

On 9th May 1939 a representative from the Architects Department visited the school to peg out the sites for the Air Raid Shelter.

Toni could not find anything interesting as she read through the book. It just seemed to be the highlights in the story of the school. Toni would have been far more interested if it had had a few more details. She would have enjoyed writing them:

Today Sandra Jones was given two hundred lines for writing, "Miss Atkin has warts on her nose," on the toilet door.
Perhaps mention of someone getting punished:
Tommy Blackstone was give five strokes of the cane because he was caught taking dinner money from the head teacher's office.
A few netball and football results would make the book better too.

Toni thumbed through the book, looking for something that might help her to find out how it had transported her back to the 1940's, but there was nothing there.
Toni turned to the last page of the book and wrote the date when she had last been in her own time. She placed the open book on her dressing table and tried spinning her special owl over it. An owl was supposed to be a talisman of wisdom, but it didn't seem to be giving her much help right now.

Should she have murmured some magic words or an incantation? Should she have dressed in white robes with laurel leaves entwined in her hair? Should she have danced in a circle round the book?

Toni thought carefully about the day she had been moved through time. She hadn't done anything; she had just opened the book at the right date and read what was written there. She had to be missing something vital: there must have been something else she had forgotten.

Toni decided to try and re-enact the whole scene. That was what the police always do when conducting an investigation, she had seen it many times on the television; they reconstruct what had happened.

Her dressing table would be the table in the school and her bed could be the blackboard, lying on its side. She put a few books around the room where she thought she could remember finding them. Then she went out of her bedroom turned round three times to clear her mind and went back in again. This time she had to pretend she was back in '*Almund Primary school.*'

Toni walked into the room, trying her best to imagine she was in the right place. She listened carefully to see if there was a teacher on the stairs. Mr Cuthbert might be about to come up, so she flattened against the wall for a moment.
Then she went into the classroom. She wandered round the room, taking the scene in. Then she rubbed her hand on her pretend blackboard and dusted the chalk from her hands.

She picked up a small book and read it a little. It had been one of the books she had first used when learning to read. Toni tried to remember what the book was about, it seemed so easy to read now.
What next? Had she missed anything important?

The old leather book was on the table, so she went over and picked it up in both hands. Toni held it in mid air. There was something wrong. Something else had happened. There had been a sound. What was it?

Toni went out of the room; she had to go through the whole thing again. The door, the books, the blackboard, the … That sound! She could hear it now. Something fell onto the table. She was trying desperately to remember what it must have been. It had fallen on the table and made a tinkling sound, like something made of silver.

That was it. It was round and silver. She could see it now, a sliver thing that was like a small Compact disk! She needed to see it. She needed to examine it and find out what it was: it was the only thing missing, A silver disk! Toni had only seen it for a few split seconds but there was something about it she seemed to know.

How could she ever find the disk again? It would mean going back into the school and hunting round for it. As far as she knew, Miss Atkin had all the books and things she needed and probably would not be going near the damaged school again.

Toni stopped, that was a stupid idea. The last time she had seen the disk, it was in the empty classroom in Almund *Primary* School. She had removed the Book from Miss Atkin's office and there had been no disk there! It could be absolutely anywhere but there was something about the disk that was shouting at her. It was at the back of her mind. Toni tried to think, but she could not recall ever seeing anything like the disk before.

There was something else that was still wrong; something she had done when she went into the room. Toni did not know what it was, but she could sense she had missed something out of her reconstruction of events. Toni put all thoughts of the silver disk out of her mind for the moment; there was something more important she had to concentrate on.

Toni went back outside and went down the stairs, trying to recall her movements, how she felt, what she saw and anything she had heard. She slowly began to climb the stairs. Edna clattered in the kitchen and the sudden noise startled Toni. She recalled there had been a sound before. Something had startled her.

Toni glanced down at her hand. Without realising what she was doing, she had taken the owl out from under her jumper and was now holding it in her hand. Toni sighed. Of course that was it! She had been holding her owl, her lucky charm, in her hand when she went into the classroom upstairs!

Toni went through the whole scene again, right up to the point where she had picked up the book. She picked it up with two hands. If she hadn't, she would not have been able to hold it open, so she must have let go of her owl. A disk was on the book. It was made from silver. She had seen it. How could she have forgotten about the disk?
Toni put down the book and searched round her room for something which could be the silver disk in her reconstruction. She found a piece of cardboard and tore it into a circle that was about the right size and then put it on the book.

Toni held on to her owl and walked towards the book then she let go of the owl and picked the book up.

"What you doing?" a voice asked from behind her.
Toni swung round to see little Tom standing in the doorway of her room. He had a puzzled expression on his face.
"What you doing, Toni? He asked again.
Toni put the book down and swept her tiny grandfather up into her arms.
"I was just playing a silly game!" Toni told him, "Shall we go to your room and see if we can find a story there?"
Little Tom liked that idea; he jumped down on to the floor and pulled Toni away.

Chapter Thirty
Silver Disk

The next day was one when Toni did not have to go to school in Tuther. She had been given a lot of homework to do by Miss Atkin and there was also a chance she might go and see Rev Thomas to ask if she could have a look at one of his books about Ancient Rome.

Edna asked Toni if she wouldn't mind taking young Tom to school for her, so she could borrow the bike to go into Tuther to see how Tom Senior was getting on in hospital. Toni happily agreed, walking all the way to school with Maureen holding onto one hand and Little Tom the other.

It was nice to see Nuther School again. It was still overcrowded with refugee children from the large cities, but the two teachers seemed to have got things better organised. There were three new adult faces on the playground she did not recognise. One of the parents told her they were teachers from some of the schools where the evacuation children came from originally. They had been sent along with the children and were in lodgings with some of the villagers.

Toni handed Little Tom over to Miss Dobson, then she took Maureen over to say 'hello' to Miss Booth who was still standing by the entrance to the school, keeping a wary eye open for any late comers.

"Good morning Miss Booth, How are you today?" Toni asked.

"I am well thank you, Toni," Miss Booth replied, "How are things at Almund School?"

"The school hasn't been repaired yet, but we are all being housed in the Parish Hall."

"It must be as crowded there as it was in here!" Miss Booth commented. "The Rev Thomas has been kind. He has cleared out one of his large rooms for the older children to use. He has even started giving a few lessons about the Romans for us himself."

The more Toni spoke to Miss Booth, the more Toni realised the voice at the back of her head was trying to tell her something.

"One of the teachers from Portsmouth, a Miss Brindle, is teaching at the vicarage and we have a Miss Carlson who takes her class up to the doctors' house. You see, anyone who has got a large room in their home is kindly allowing us to 'expand' the school, far beyond our normal boundaries!"

The voice in Toni's head was now jumping up and down and banging its fists on the side of Toni's skull, trying to get her attention, but she was too busy chattering to notice.

"That sounds wonderful, Miss Booth, it's alright at Almund School, but it is a bother getting there every day. It also means Edna can't get into the hospital when I have the bike!"

"Oh yes, I heard all about poor Tom! I understand you helped?"

The voice was now shouting through a megaphone. Toni stopped talking and slowly looked up at Miss Booth, her eyes wide open.

"Your necklace has a silver disk on it!" She seemed to be murmuring the words as if she was in some kind of weird trance.

Miss Booth was concerned, "Yes dear, you examined it in class."

Something hit Toni hard in the chest. A thump of her heart sent a pulse racing through her. Miss Booth was wearing the silver disk she had seen. Her owl must have touched it when she picked up the book.

No! That was wrong. When she read the book it had been about what had happened the day the bomb fell on the school. She must have done something else.

Miss Booth was watching Toni, wondering why she was standing so still and silent.

That was it! She had picked up the silver disc to look at it. There had been a flash of lightening! Her owl had touched it!

Toni understood everything now.

She took Maureen by the hand and began to lead her away but then she stopped, she had to talk to Miss Booth: she needed to tell her everything.

"Can I come and see you sometime soon please Miss Booth? There is something important I need to tell you." Toni sounded strangely excited.

Miss Booth was surprised and confused.

"Of course you can Toni, come anytime you like! You know where I live!"

Toni turned, nodding her head and smiling. She then took Maureen with her to visit Rev Thomas, hoping he wasn't too busy to let her look at some of his books.

Rev Thomas showed Toni and Maureen into his own personal study. Toni could hear a lesson taking place in another room because the children were reciting multiplication tables.

"Have you seen Miss Booth's necklace?" Toni asked him.

"I have not only seen it, Toni, but I have also been able to find a picture of something that is much like it." Rev Thomas went to his bookshelf and lifted down a thin book which he opened in front of her.

"There is an owl in the middle of it; it looks just like the one I found!" Toni declared, "Could I make a copy of it?"

"That is a good idea. Are you any good at drawing?"

Rev Thomas fetched some paper and pencils. He also had some colouring pencils he gave to little Maureen so she would have something to do whilst Toni was busy.

"Sometimes, I find you only really see a thing when you draw it," he explained, "When you look at something, you never take in all the details, that's why drawing it is such a good idea."

Toni had to agree, she loved drawing and, much to Rev Thomas surprise, she was good at it too. She took care to draw the outline of the disk faintly first only putting in the details and shading once she had got it perfect.

Maureen was busy with her colouring; she had drawn a house with huge flowers all over the garden, and a tree with apples and bird's nests all over it. But for the war, Maureen would probably have been able to start school. In her own time, Toni knew Maureen would have been to Nursery School every day.

Toni finished her picture and copied some of the information she had found out. It was a silver copy of an ancient Roman amulet. The book explained it was dedicated to the goddess Minerva, but Toni preferred to use the Greek name of Athena.

Toni finished her picture, ready to show it to Miss Atkin when she went to school on the next day. She wondered what she should tell Miss Booth though; she needed to learn more about the silver disk. Perhaps it would be better if she just sat down and told Miss Booth the whole story, missing nothing out. She might believe Toni or she might think she had gone totally mad; there was no way to tell. All Toni knew was that the secret to her return could be hanging around Miss Booth's neck.

There was one thing bothering her. The bomb had not killed anyone. Miss Booth was not Almund School's head teacher and Tom was still alive. She had changed history. Could she have changed it for the worse as well as for the better?

Toni walked back to the Braithwaite's house, wondering how she was going to keep Maureen occupied with all the turmoil that was going on inside her head. The back door was wide open. Toni was sure she had closed it before she left. Inside the kitchen the kettle was on, it was just starting to bubble away. It hadn't been there when she left. Something caught her eye. Her bike was leaning against the shed door. It could only mean one thing: Edna was home.

Toni walked through to the front room with Maureen, wondering how Edna had managed to get to and from the hospital so quickly. There was a surprise for them both when they went into the room.

Old Tom was there. He was sitting in his favourite chair while Edna fussed around, looking for his slippers.

"They discharged Tom this morning," Edna told her, "Then we were lucky to get a lift all the way home in the postman's van. I had to sit in the back with the bike and all the heavy parcels he was delivering to Wether. But it was ok; much better than having to wait for a bus!"

Toni was delighted and went over to give Tom senior a huge hug.

Tom held her tight, "I have been told if it had not been for what you did for me, Edna would have been left here on her own!"

Toni did not know what to say. She couldn't think of a simple explanation so she let her silence speak for its self.

"You know Toni, we owe everything to you. One day you will get your memory back and be reunited with your family, but whatever happens in the future, you have to know you will always be important to us."

Toni was near to tears; she put her arms around Tom and gave him a big hug.

Chapter Thirty One
Miss Booth

Toni knocked gently on Miss Booth's door. Half of her wanted the lady to be out; the other half was excited about what she was about to do. Toni waited a few seconds, and when she didn't see a light or any movement in the hallway, she turned and began to go back down the short garden path.

It was a dark night with no moon, so the blackout, intended to keep enemy bombers confused, made it difficult for Toni to find out where she was going. Tom had a special torch called a 'number eight' which he only used sparingly. It shone light down on the ground without spreading it in a wide beam. He had said Toni could use it, but only after she had stood in the dark for a few minutes to let her eyes get used to the darkness. The torch was designed to light the road but it didn't shine like any torch Toni had seen before. She thought it was actually quite useless, giving out less light than a flickering candle which was about to go out.

Toni was amazed at how wonderful the sky was. Where she had lived, there were many street lamps and car head lights caused the starlight to be greatly diminished. Now the whole of the Milky Way lay above her, in a beautiful stream of tiny stars.

Toni wished she had listened to her teachers at school when they had told her about the planets that circled the sun. They were somewhere up there now, but she did not have any idea which one was which. The only thing she could recall was the constellation of 'Orion' which she had been shown many times. Orion's sword now stood out brighter than she had ever seen it.

Toni turned to hear a call from inside the house.

"Is that you Toni? I don't want to put the light on! Come along inside."

Toni's heart started to beat quickly She wanted to run away, forget all about it, but she forced herself to go inside Miss Booth's house. Once inside she could relax and tell her story: there would be no going back.

Toni was settled in a large, comfortable arm chair. The chair's owner was cross at being disturbed, so she immediately jumped back up onto Toni's lap, stretched her claws and fell asleep with a gentle purring.

Miss Booth made them both a cup of tea which was accompanied by a large slice of cake.

"You shouldn't have!" Toni smirked,"That is a big slice!"

"I made it yesterday, if you do not eat it, it will only go to waste."

Toni took a large bite; it was as good as it appeared to be. The ladies at the library would have approved it!

"There was something you wanted to tell me, wasn't there Toni?"

Toni took a deep breath, where to begin? How could she convince the lady she was telling her the truth and not just making up fanciful ideas?

"Miss Booth, you know what happened to Tom?"

"Yes Toni, I heard all about that! It sounds absolutely amazing; I didn't know it was possible!"

"I was taught how to do it."

Miss Booth gave her a hard look.

"I was taught how to do that at school. Everyone in my class was."

"In school? Which school was that, I didn't know any schools would know about it - I certainly didn't?"

"It was Almund School."

Miss Booth was finding it difficult to believe.

"Almund School?"

"Almund Primary School to be exact!"

"When did it change its name? I didn't read about anything in the papers?"

"It hasn't changed its name, "Toni took a deep breath, "but it will!"

"There is something you are trying to tell me, Toni. You are going round in circles and confusing me; you need to spit it out and get it over with." Miss Booth was looking cross.

"If I tell you, you have to understand I am telling the truth. I am not making things up."

"I think I know you well enough by now to know you are not a silly girl! You have come out here in the dark to talk to me, so I know it has to be important."

"You know a bomb exploded on the shelter of Almund School?"

"Yes of course and I saw your picture in the paper too."

"I knew it was going to happen."

"You knew? How did you know?"

"In the same way I knew about Cardio pulmonary resuscitation, I am not from here. I am from the future – Two thousand and thirteen to be precise!"

Miss Booth slumped back in her chair and let out a gasp of surprise.

"How else would I know about something even our own doctor has never heard about? It hasn't been discovered yet, it won't be -for a few years to come."

"Tell me how it happened, Toni." Miss Booth leaned forward, her cup of tea balanced in her lap, listening attentively.

Toni told her the whole story. She started with why they had all got dressed up in the right clothes, and then how she had gone upstairs to the unused classrooms in the school. Finally she told Miss Booth about how she had told them all to run out of the air raid shelter.

"I read all about that, I thought at the time you must know something no one else did. Now I know why." The lady looked intently at Toni. Miss Booth had something that she needed to know, but didn't know how to ask.

"You are English aren't you Toni? I have been thinking that you have a slightly strange accent?"

Toni wanted to laugh, but she realised that Miss Booth was only trying to find out what was a very important fact in those days.

"Yes Miss Booth, I am English, and yes we did win the war, though it was a long time before I was born."

Miss Booth jumped out of her chair, "We won? Are you sure? We defeated the Germans?"

If Miss Booth had known about 'punching the air in delight' she would have done that now.

"Yes! Germany was defeated. Hitler died and the terrible Nazis were no more" Toni told her, "But I have been thinking about some other things."

"Go on?" Miss Booth didn't know what could be more important.

"Well, Tom should have died, shouldn't he?"

"Yes! If you had not been there, he certainly would. That thing you did saved him."

"So I have changed history. I have done something that made the world different."

"But it was only to one person. One person won't make such a huge difference."

"No Miss Booth, the bomb on the air raid shelter should have killed over thirty people, teachers and children, but I stopped it happening: they all survived."

"They could have escaped?"

"But they didn't, we have been remembering what happened to them for the last seventy years! Those children will all be grown up; they have probably had children too. History has been changed a lot. If I could go back, it might all be different."

"You mean because you have **changed history here, it could in some strange way effect the final outcome of the war?"**

Toni thought about it for a while, and then she began to speak.

"There could be someone who should have taken part in the fighting they might have been replaced by someone else."

"How do you mean?" Miss Booth was listening.

"Well suppose that person did not do what they should have done. They missed their target, they went the wrong way. It could have made things different. We could have lost because of me!"

Toni was slowly realising what she might have caused, she was near to tears again.
"I have only been here a short time, but I might have done a lot of damage already."
"I see what you mean, the longer you stay here in the wrong time; the more dangerous it is for us in the future. You might not have done any damage yet, but the longer you stay here, the greater the threat must be."

Toni was surprised Miss Booth not only understood she was from the future, but also that it was vitally important for her to go back.

"I don't understand how you came to travel here; you haven't mentioned anything about a 'time machine'?"

"It wasn't like that; it was as if I 'fell through time' to be here. One second it was normal then the next I was here, being dragged by Rose down to the shelter."

"You must have done something? Something must have made it happen."

"I have tried to think about it a lot. I even pretended I was back in the school and walked through the whole thing until I think I got it right. That is really why I came to see you."

"Me!" Miss Booth was surprised, "What have I got to do with it?"

Toni had to do some careful explaining and hoped she could be tactful and not offend the teacher.
"You know the year I lived in was 2013?" Toni was saying.
"Yes, of course, though I can't imagine what it must be like so far into the future!"
"That's over seventy years off; I don't know how old you are Miss Booth but ..."
"I am 48 Toni, if you really want to know!"

Toni did a quick calculation in her head.
"It would mean that in my time you are nearly 120 years old!"
"It's sweet of you to be so kind Toni, but I think I understand! In your time, I, and all my friends, are long gone!"

Toni smiled; she had never had to tell someone that they were dead before.
"The school log book was on a table and I think your necklace was lying on top of it."
"My necklace? How could it get there? I have never been inside Almund School."

Toni had more to tell her.
"But you did!"
Miss Booth's eyes were wide open.
"You remember how I told you they were all killed when the bomb exploded on top of the air raid shelter?"
"Yes, but what has ..."
"Miss Atkin was killed too,"
"Oh, I see."

"So they needed a new head teacher to take her place, to run the school during the war. From what I have discovered, I think you took over from her and went to run the school."
"What me! The head teacher of a huge school like Almund!"
"That is how your necklace came to be on top of the log book."
"I would have thought something as important as the log book would be in the head teacher's office!"
"I think it stopped being used a few years ago. I don't think head teachers write a log book anymore, or perhaps they had a newer one! Anyway it was there, upstairs in that room."
"Alright, go on then, Toni."

"I have got an old owl necklace which I have round my neck all the time."
"Yes, I know about that, you found it in the woods didn't you?"
"That is nearly right, you see I have worked it out that Tom and Edna Braithwaite are actually my own great grandparents, and their son, little Tom, is my grandpa!"

Miss Booth was helpless with laughter. There were tears streaming down her face. It was all just too much for her to take in.
"Toni this is just amazing, it's a fantastic story!"
"It's not a story: it's true!"
"Yes, yes, I know, it's a true story, but it is so funny. You have been babysitting your own grandfather!"
Toni saw the funny side of it and began to laugh as well.

When they had calmed down, Toni was able to carry on with her story.
"I originally found the owl under a loose floorboard in my grandfather's house - I used to go there to visit them a lot during the holidays - but I lost it when the bomb exploded."

"Let me get this right. You found it in the woods and then lost it when the bomb exploded? I am confused."

"It is confusing; I know in your time, I found it in the wood, - that's right, but in my time, I know I found it under the floorboard - that's right too! Someone must have put it in my Grandfather's house for me to find in the future; then I lost it when the bomb exploded.

"I think when the bomb exploded you left it behind. It will still be there."

"If I ever manage to go back to my own time, will I ever find it?

"From what you are saying, it looks as though the owl cannot travel through time!"

"Why didn't the owl come with me?"

"It's the key Toni; it's the thing that opens the door! What we don't know is what the lock is!"

"Oh, I think I do." Toni explained. "I think the disk around your neck is the lock. When I picked the log book up, my owl was dangling round my neck and must have touched your disk."

Miss Booth sat back, with a glimmer of understanding in her eyes: the tale was slowly getting pieced together.

Chapter Thirty Two
Plans

It was time for tea and some more of Miss Booth's cake.

They sat drinking their tea, talking about everything and anything apart from the one thing that really mattered. Miss Booth was an interesting lady who had lived through two world wars. She had experienced a lot of both sadness and joy in her life, though now she knew this terrible war would end one day, she was far more optimistic than she had ever been before.

Eventually Miss Booth decided they had to talk about the 'really important thing': their very own, 'Elephant in the room!'

"We have to get you back to your time, Toni, before anything else happens that will damage history. Even the fact that I know how it all ends could make a difference. I might do something or tell someone something that will cause changes to happen."

Toni agreed.

"I think all I have to do is to touch my owl against your necklace and I will go back to where I come from."

Miss Booth thought about things for a minute.

"If you are right you would just vanish. No one would know where you are. People would go looking for you. There would be a huge search."

Toni took a deep breath.

"The last place I was seen would be here with you. The police would think you had done something to me!"

"Oh no! What would I tell them then? She was here, but she has just popped back to 2013 to do some shopping for me - she will be back in a minute or two!"

Toni laughed, but it was true it was going to look very suspicious. They had to make plans, careful plans, so Toni could vanish without anyone knowing.

"Let's not rush into things, let's sleep on it. You go home and try to think up some ideas. I will do the same and then we can meet in a few days and plan out all the details. We don't want to go upsetting everyone."

Toni struggled to walk the short distance home. Miss Booth offered to walk with her but Toni did not see the sense in them both getting lost in the dark. She had her torch, so that would help, but she only used it sparingly.

The worst part was when she startled to walk past the church next to Rev Thomas's Vicarage. Toni did not believe in ghosts or anything like that but as she walked along the road by the side of the graveyard, a loud screech made her blood run cold. Something flashed overhead, vanishing into the woods beyond. Toni stopped, her heart beating fiercely. It was an owl! She told herself the owl was out hunting for its supper; there was nothing to worry about but she ran quickly onward.

As she stepped off the narrow pavement, she remembered what Tom had told her.

"Always listen carefully before you cross a road. Sometimes a car can be upon you in the dark before you realise it is there." Toni had, for once, been listening! The number of serious accidents and even fatalities that had happened since the blackout started, had gone up dramatically, especially in the large towns and cities.

Toni lay in bed in her room in the Braithwaite's house wondering how she could go back to her own time without anyone realising she had vanished. It was bad enough having her Mum and the rest of her family wondering where she was. Toni did not want to upset any more of the lovely people who had come into her life. But 'how to do it' was the big question. Miss Booth would help of course; she might even come up with a good plan.

"If only I could just go back to my Mum," Toni thought to herself, a tear starting to form in the corner of her eye. She sat up in bed! Perhaps that was it: she could pretend to go home. She could tell all her friends that her Mum had come to take her back and then vanish.

As she went over it in her mind, she could see it had huge flaws. How did her Mum know she was alright in the first place? Toni thought about it. Then slowly a better plan formed in her mind.

Miss Booth would write a letter to the local paper, supposedly from Toni's Mum, asking them to pass it on to Toni. The letter would say they had heard about her from a friend and her family had moved to a village quite far away because of the bombing. There would be a train ticket in the letter and an address in a village she was to go to. Mum would say she could not come and collect her because her sister was ill and had to be cared for, or something like that.

It gave Toni a reason for going and a chance to say goodbye to them all. But she would have to actually get on the train herself and leave with her bag. That was a problem. Maybe she could just go a few stations down the line and meet up with Miss Booth and then vanish. Miss Booth could find a way to get into her bedroom at the Braithwaite's house and hide the owl under the floor boards, so Toni could find it herself, back in her own time.

Toni found a piece of paper next morning and carefully wrote out the letter she wanted Miss Booth to copy.

Dearest Toni

You cannot believe how happy we are you are alright. A friend of mine that lives near Tuther sent me the newspaper that had your picture in it. I am so proud of everything that you have done.

I am sorry I cannot come to Tuther to get you, my sister Cath is ill, I have to stay here to look after her. I will put a train ticket in with this letter so that you can come back to us straightaway. I am posting this letter on Monday, if everything goes well, you should get this letter soon after it arrives at the newspaper office in Tuther. I shall be waiting for you at the station on Saturday morning. If you do not come that day for any reason I shall make sure that someone is there every day to meet you and bring you to our house.

I am overjoyed to know that you are safe.

Mum xxx

Later that day, Toni showed the letter to Miss Booth and explained her escape plan to her. Miss Booth listened to Toni carefully. She thought it was an excellent plan; it should be quite an easy thing for them to pull off. However there was one detail that needed to be changed.

"Every letter has a postmark on the stamp," Miss Booth told her, "We need to be careful about where the letter is posted. If it is posted in Tuther, the newspaper people will notice that and get suspicious about whom the letter is really from. "

Toni was crestfallen; she wondered how many other details she had forgotten.

"But don't worry, Toni. " Miss Booth patted her hand, "I can catch the train into a different town on Sunday. I can say I am going to see a friend. Then I can post the letter for you. We can change the date too, to make it sound totally convincing. They will think you are going back to your Mum, which is of course is exactly what you are going to be doing. You won't even be telling lies to all your friends!"

Toni clapped her hands in delight. There were so many other problems she didn't want to even begin to think about.

What if the key that opened the lock was not her 'owl'?

What if the silver disk round Miss Booth's neck wasn't the lock after all?

And what if she didn't get taken back home!

What if she was transported to a time or to a place she did not know?

There was so much to worry about, but she would not know if the plan actually worked until they tried it out. There was going to be no trial run or rehearsal with this one.

Chapter Thirty Three

Plans

Miss Booth had set out all their plans carefully numbering each stage in the plan so they would both know what to do.

1. Miss Booth would copy out the letter.
2. On Sunday morning Miss Booth would catch the train to Reading where she could visit a friend.
3. Toni must remain calm; when the letter finally arrives she must behave excitedly not giving anything away.
4. Toni must rush home as quickly as she can with the good news and burst into the house to tell Tom and Edna about the letter. They must be convinced it is real.
5. Toni must then plan her trip to Reading where she is going to be met. Tom and Edna and a few others will want to go to see her off, but Miss Booth won't be there.
6. Toni will get on the train to Reading but she will get off at Ulverton where Miss Booth will be waiting for her.
7. Toni will touch the owl onto the silver disk and return home.
8. If the owl remains behind, Miss Booth will find an opportunity in the next few years to put the owl under the floor board. Toni has told her exactly where it is.

Toni wanted to write, 'This message will self destruct on Sunday.' But Miss Booth could not see the funny side of her suggestion, no matter how hard Toni tried.

"I am being serious now Toni, it is vitally important no one ever sees this list. I would suggest you read it and learn it."

"Do you think I should eat it after I have read it?" Toni asked.

Miss Booth gave her a serious 'over the top of the glasses' look.

*

There was a sombre mood in school when Toni arrived on her bike a few mornings later. Lizzy apparently knew all about it, from her father, but she had decided to stay quiet and not say anything, not really believing her father's report had been true.

The children were kept waiting for more than twenty minutes before the doors were finally opened by Miss Hodgness. She was a young teacher and seemed to be pale and shocked. As the children came into the hall, they were told to come and sit on the floor so they could be given some important information.

"What is it?" Toni asked, whispering in Lizzy's ear.
"Don't" Lizzy simply said, Toni could tell she was upset.
Miss Hodgness was pushed forward by the other teachers; they had obviously decided she would be the spokesman.

"Children,"
She stopped and searched round for her colleagues' support, heads nodded telling her to carry on.
"I am sorry to tell you we have just received some terrible news." She stopped speaking again taking out a white handkerchief from her sleeve to wipe away a tear.
"I don't know what we are going to do, but..." She had to stop again, "Miss Atkin met with an awful accident last night,"

As her voice tailed away, children struggled to hear what she was saying. ,

"I am sorry to be the one the one to tell you, but she has died. There was nothing the doctors could do."

"Miss Atkin is dead!" Toni could not believe what she was hearing.

"Yes, Dad told me early this morning." Lizzy explained, "It seems she tripped over the edge of a step and fell into the road."

"That's horrendous."

"She didn't stand a chance, she was lying in the road when a car...." Lizzy made a disgusting face.

All around children were in tears. Some were comforted by their teachers, others just sat in silence, stunned by the news. Miss Atkin had been a teacher everyone had the deepest respect for.

Captain Carter appeared in the room. He was red faced and obviously very angry.

"I need to speak with Miss Atkin this minute!" He announced paying no attention to the scene of distress before him.

"At once! This minute if you please!"

Miss Hodgness pulled herself up to her full height.

"Get out, you odious little man, before I summon the police to escort you away."

Captain Carter was speechless.

"One more word from you, you trumpeted up little Hitler and I will not be responsible for my actions, now go away!"

The Captain knew when he was beaten and fled for the door.

"Who is going to be the headteacher now?" Lizzy was asking, "None of the others look like they know how to run a school. They will soon be in a real flap. They are going to need some help- and quickly!"

Toni heard herself speaking, without realising what she was saying.

"I suppose they will bring in someone from one of the small village schools. They will need a teacher who has run a school before."

Lizzy nodded, Toni was making remarkable sense.

There was a stranger at the door. It seemed he had knocked but no one was paying him any attention.

"Excuse me." The man spoke, daring to take a step further into the room.

He would never have got that far when Miss Atkin was here, Toni thought to herself.

"Excuse me. I need to speak to the headteacher." Teachers questioned each other. Miss Hodgness was given strong looks but she shook her head and turned away. One of the mothers who had agreed to help out in the school came forward. She wasn't in charge, but for now she would just have to do.

"Can I help you, I am sorry but our head teacher has been... She is not here."

The man stepped forward; glad someone was going to listen.

"A letter has been delivered to our newspaper for a Miss Toni Braithwaite. Is she perhaps a pupil at this school? We do not have any other information about her."

Miss Hodgness had only been half listening, "I am sorry! This is a difficult time for us all just now. We do not have a pupil of that name here."

The man began to turn away and walk towards the door. Someone else had heard.

"Toni Braithwaite! Of course we have, she is somewhere over there!"

The man searched around.

"Is there a Toni Braithwaite here? I have a letter for her; it was sent to the newspaper's office."

Toni was pushed forward. For a second or two she wondered what this letter was all about. The sad news concerning Miss Atkin had made her forget about the plan. Toni wasn't a good actress, so stepping forward to receive a letter she was supposed to know nothing about, made her very uncomfortable.

"A letter for me? How strange?" Toni could have been playing a part in a bad pantomime.

The newspaper man held out the envelope, wondering who this strange child was.

Toni slit the letter open with her finger and took out the plain sheet of paper.

"I wonder what this is all about." Toni had to stop herself from waving the letter in the air.

"Let me read it!" stated Miss Hodgness, coming over and pulling herself together. She wasn't sure if Toni could actually manage to read a letter on her own; perhaps the girl needed some help.

Toni came to her senses, she had to try harder with her acting or she would be about to give the entire game away.

"Oh, Oh Miss Hodgness, I can't believe it, I really can't! This is absolutely amazing! Please Miss Hodgness read it out for me."

Miss Hodgness was glad to be able to read something had some good news in it.

"Dearest Toni

You cannot believe how happy we all are, now that we know you are alright. A friend of mine that lives near Tuther sent me the newspaper. I could not stop shaking when I saw your picture in it. I am so proud of everything that you have done.

Toni it is from your mother!"

"I know, I know, isn't it amazing!"

Miss continued to read.

"I am so sorry but I cannot come to Tuther to get you, my sister Cath is ill, I have to stay here to look after her.

That's sad Toni, I am sure she really wants to be here with you, but there is good news."

"Please tell me Miss!"

"I will put a train ticket in with this letter so that you can come back to us straightaway. I am posting this letter on Monday, if everything goes well you should get this letter soon after it arrives at the newspaper office in Tuther.

"It's Wednesday today, It hasn't taken long to find me, when is the ticket for? Have I missed it?"

"No Toni you haven't, listen:

I shall be waiting for you at the station on Saturday morning. If you do not come that day for any reason, I shall make sure that someone is there every day to meet you and bring you to our house."

I am overjoyed to know that you are safe.

Mum xxx

"Oh that is so nice," Toni thought, realising that *nice* was not quite the word she needed.

Toni sat down and carried on with the work she was doing, glad the first part of their plan had been achieved. Miss Hodgness was staring down at her.

"You surprise me Toni, I would have thought you would be running round the room in excitement, but you sound like someone who has just found sixpence after losing a shilling!"

Toni went cold, "It, it's Miss Atkin! I can't stop thinking about her." She shuddered, hoping her excuse would strike a chord.

"I wonder if you would you like to go home, Toni? I am sure we wouldn't mind you missing school for just one day after getting such exciting news.

Toni grasped at the chance; the further she was away from school, the less likely she was of give the game away.

The newspaper man was waiting outside the parish hall. He had a nose for a good story and was prepared to hang around for a while. As Toni came out of the door he took his chance to quickly interview the lucky girl.

Toni let him see the letter and waited while he made a few notes in his book. Toni really did not know what to say. The shock of Miss Atkin's' fatal accident made everything else seem so unimportant. The local journalist thought he had enough information to write something for the paper. It was going to be an interesting edition with a happy and a sad story side by side on the front page. It didn't matter if Toni couldn't think of anything to say, he was experienced enough to be able to make it all up for her.

Chapter Thirty Four
Head

As Toni was cycling down Tuther High Street she spotted Miss Booth getting out of a big black car. She had two men in suits with her. Miss Booth saw her too and waved, but she was obviously too busy to stop and chat. The three were last seen going into the council offices.

Toni cycled quickly back to Nuther, rehearsing what she was going to do and say over and over in her mind. She had not been concentrating in school and had made a real mess of things. When she got to the Braithwaite's house she was going to be convincing.

Toni had her scene rehearsed and perfected. She was word perfect; she knew exactly what she was going to say. She parked her bike at the side of the house and burst in through the front door shouting,
"Tom! Edna! You will never believe what has happened!"

Toni ran into the front room to shout her good news once more, but stopped dead in her tracks when she saw a policeman sitting talking to Tom and Edna. He had a cup of tea balanced on his knee.

A million thoughts surged through Toni's mind.
They know about the letter, they have found the plan,

They want to know about CPR,

They want to ask me about that boy I threw into the bins,

They know I am from the future,

 They have caught me; I will never get home now.

"Hello Toni!" Tom spoke first, "You are home from school early!"

Toni suddenly felt guilty, as if she had been personally responsible for the bomb and Miss Atkin's accident as well.

"I got a letter," Toni mumbled.

The policeman stood up, thanked Edna for the tea and headed for the door. He could tell when he was not wanted anymore.

"Constable Bill is an old friend of mine, "Tom told her, "He was just passing and called in to see how I was getting on"

A likely story Toni thought, *they have been talking about me behind my back, they all know something but won't tell me.*

"You got a letter Toni? Who is it from?"

Toni remembered her practised script. Only seeing the policeman had put her off, her performance was way below the standard she had planned.

"It's from my Mum, Tom, she saw my picture in the paper and she has sent me a ticket."

She wasn't explaining things well so Tom took the proffered letter and read it for himself.

"This is wonderful news Toni. It looks like you will be leaving us on Saturday morning! "

Edna took the letter and read it too.

"Are you sure, absolutely sure this letter is from your mother Toni?"

"Of course I am!" Toni was staring round the room. Was something amiss?

"This handwriting is distinctive, I am sure I have seen it before, it is so perfectly written."

"Mum writes beautifully."

"This is the handwriting of someone who is well educated, a teacher or lawyer perhaps. Does your Mum work?"

"Yes, she does, I just remembered she, she is a bank manager!" Toni blurted out the information without thinking.

"There cannot be many ladies who are bank managers Toni; she must be an important lady. It is a wonder I have not heard of her before."

A little lie, quickly told, was digging Toni into a deep hole from which she was going to have difficulty getting out.

"Did I say Bank manager; I think I meant she works in a bank. Yes that's it she works in a bank. She does the cleaning!" Toni was starting to stutter and stammer it was obvious she was not telling an ounce of truth.

"That memory of yours is still mixed up isn't it?" Edna smiled kindly.

"You will have to start packing." Tom explained. "I will ask the postman if he will give you a lift to the station in Uther on Saturday morning."

"Uther?" Toni wondered, "Is there a station there?"

"Oh yes. It's much better to get the train from Uther, it is much nearer."

Edna butted in, "But if she gets the one from Tuther it is a direct train! It doesn't stop at any of the stations, it goes straight to Reading."

Tom had a book open. It says here the 8:45 from Tuther goes straight through, you are right. The next one isn't until 9:30 and it stops everywhere!"

"Does it stop at Uther too?" Toni asked.

"No, that's on a different line, it doesn't go anywhere near Uther."

She wanted to ask if the train from Uther went through Ulverton but didn't dare ask.

"It would be much better if she gets the 8:45 from Tuther, then." Tom agreed. Toni breathed a sigh of relief: the whole plan had been on the point of collapse for a moment there.

"I can catch the bus into Tuther on Saturday morning."

"It leaves here at six! Do you think you can manage to get up in time?"

"I am going home to my Mum! I will stay up all night if I have to." This time Toni did sound convincing.

Tom was looking at Edna; they were both smiling and obviously had an idea of their own. Toni went up to her room to begin to sort through some things. She did not have a lot. All she owned could probably be wrapped up in a simple, brown paper parcel.

She hadn't been there long when she heard someone at the door. Edna called for her to come downstairs. Miss Booth had come to see her. It was only as she reached the door to the sitting room she remembered she would have to tell Miss Booth about the letter she had received.

"Miss Booth, has Edna told you my good news?" Toni announced as she came in.

"I heard about it in Almund School." Miss Booth answered.

"Almund School? Have you been there?"

"Two men from the Local Education Board called to see me this morning. They had some bad news. I believe you were told about it at school this morning?"

"You mean poor Miss Atkin?"

Edna butted in, "You didn't say anything about Miss Atkin, Toni."

Toni realised she had forgotten to tell the sad news, in her enthusiasm to get her story about the letter right.

"It's sad," Toni told Edna, "Poor Miss Atkin had a dreadful accident in Tuther."

"Is she going to be alright?"

Miss Booth and Toni both shook their heads; Edna looked sadly down at the floor.

"I thought it was sudden and, if you don't mind me saying so, disrespectful, but the two men who came to see me were adamant in their request. They say if something is not done immediately then Almund School will be in great difficulty."

"What do you mean?" Edna was asking.

"They have asked me to take over as the head teacher of Almund School!" Miss Booth explained.

Toni was astounded, "That means that history ..."

Miss Booth stopped her dead in her tracks, "Yes! History lessons will be back on the timetable! Toni!"

Edna and Tom wondered what they meant, but both failed to understand what the two were talking about.

"What about our own school?" Tom asked.

"Miss Dobson is going to be in charge for now, Miss Hodgness is being moved there to be her assistant and teach the older children. I think it will be a good move for them both."

Toni was smiling; she couldn't see the frail Miss Hodgness coping with all those unruly evacuation children in Nuther's school, though she would have a lot of help from the teachers who had now arrived.

Chapter Thirty Five
Newspaper

On Friday morning Tom received their weekly newspaper through the door. He was surprised to see Toni's picture on the front page again. The headline read:

Local Hero to be Reunited

Thanks to this paper's coverage of her story, Toni Braithwaite, a pupil at Almund School, is to be finally reunited with her family. Toni, who suffered serious memory loss as the result of an exploding bomb, personally led children from her school to safety, seconds before an enemy bomb impacted on the shelter.

Toni not only rescued many children from her school, she also helped to save the life of Mr Thomas Braithwaite with whom she has lodged since the explosion.

Toni's picture was seen in this paper by her mother when a friend sent a copy to her. Toni will be leaving Tuther for Reading by train on Saturday morning. We are sure that best wishes for her future from the whole of Tuther will surely travel with her.

Blackout Fatality

We have to report the sad loss of Miss Agnes Atkin, former head teacher of Almund School, who was fatally injured last Saturday evening, when she apparently tripped over a step and fell into the path of an oncoming vehicle. Police Constable Gregg who attended the scene of the accident reported that there was little that the driver of the vehicle could have done. It was a very dark night, a total blackout was in force and Miss Atkin fell in front of the vehicle so quickly that the driver was unable to swerve out of the way. The name of the driver has been withheld by the police under the circumstances.

Miss Atkin was a much loved and respected head teacher who has valiantly served this community for many years. She will be sadly missed by all at Almund School.

In their determination to find a swift replacement for Miss Atkin, the Tuther Local Education Board have today announced that Miss Booth, currently head teacher of Nuther School, will take over, with immediate effect. They apologised for the swiftness of their decision but feel that lingering over an appointment would prove to be damaging for everyone involved with Almund School. Almund School is currently housed in the Parish Hall where lessons are continuing under extreme pressure. The Local Education Board has assured this paper that this is not acceptable and that repairs to Almund School will begin with the greatest urgency.

"I have never ever had my picture in the paper," Tom declared, "Yet you have had two stories written about you on the front page!"

Toni smiled, this was the kind of exposure she would really rather not have. Toni should have been attending Almund School that day, but Tom and Edna thought she should spend the day saying goodbye to all the friends whom she had made since her arrival.

Toni was also worried she might miss the bus into Tuther, but the Braithwaite's told her she should not worry about that.

The first person Toni set off to see was Nanny Botley. She took little Tom and Maureen with her as she walked with them to Wether.

Nanny Botley was out in her garden, tending to her vegetable patch. For a lady of quite advanced years, she was still managing to grow most of the food she needed and often had enough left over to supply vegetables for quite a few of her neighbours. Tom and Maureen ran off to be with their nanny's animals and play in her garden.

Although Toni liked Nanny Botley, she really wanted to find out how Godfrey was getting on in the shop with Mr Rodgers. She need not have worried. Godfrey had settled into the job quickly. Mr Rodgers was delighted to see Toni when she called in at the shop.

"I would never have thought the likes of him would be any use to anyone, but he has been worth his weight in gold since you persuaded me to take him on! That is a lot of gold, I can tell you!"

Toni giggled; Godfrey certainly was a big lad.

"We almost had tears last week! All I wanted to do was to put his apron in the wash so it would be clean, but he would not let me have it. I had to go out and buy another one for him to wear! He thinks that apron is the absolute best thing he has ever owned."

Toni hoped Mr Rodgers was paying Godfrey for all the work he was doing.

"I don't actually pay Godfrey, he doesn't understand money and it confuses him. So I send him home every night with something special for his Mum. Then when his Mum comes into the shop, I give her the money he has earned. I think Godfrey will still be working here when the war is over. He never grumbles, he is never late and he is polite and courteous to all of my customers. As far as I am concerned he is the absolute ideal employee!"

Toni was delighted Godfrey was doing so well. What would be even more fantastic, would be for Mr Rodgers to spread the word to other shopkeepers. There were many handicapped people like Godfrey who deserved to be given a chance.

On the way home from Nanny Botley's, Toni called in to see Rev Thomas who was happy to see her. He had read about her letter in the paper too and he was delighted she had finally found out where her family was.

"I think when the war is over, which, please God, it will be one day, I will try to find a team of people to excavate the area of the woods where you found that owl of yours. I would not be surprised to find other things around the area. People often went into the woods to bury their most valuable items when there was a threat of attack. Perhaps that is what happened in this case."

Toni had hoped she would be able to call in and have a final word or two with Miss Booth. There was a chance they might have to make a few final adjustments to their plans in order for them to run smoothly, but Miss Booth was not in when Toni called. She imagined the poor lady was still stuck in Tuther, trying to sort out the school, so Toni took a tired Maureen and Tom home. It had been a long day for the two little ones.

Chapter Thirty Six
Saturday

If she had been asked, Toni could not really say she was up early on Saturday morning because she did not actually go to bed! She was so excited she packed and repacked her things at least ten times before wrapping and then un-wrapping them again, in more brown paper. When she eventually staggered downstairs, carrying all that she owned in the world tucked under her arm, she found Tom and Edna were not even up yet.

"If we do not get a move on soon!" Toni shouted up the stairs, "I will miss the bus to Tuther. It leaves at six!"

A bleary eyed Tom stood at the top of the stairs. It was taking him a few minutes to gather his thoughts together.

"Sorry Toni, I forgot to tell you last night," he rubbed his eyes back into focus, "Dr Roberts said he will be going into Tuther this morning. He has offered to take you in himself."

Toni slumped down into a chair. The thought of riding into Tuther in Dr Roberts' car was lovely, but it meant she would probably have to wait at least two hours before he arrived.

Toni put her hand inside her jumper to check her special owl was still there. But it had gone!

"Where is my owl? Toni shouted, dashing up the stairs as quickly as she could. She could remember taking it off and putting it on the dressing table when she went up the night before. She even thought she had put it round her neck the first thing this morning, but it was nowhere to be seen.

Toni could feel there was something round her neck. When she searched, she found the leather string the Owl hung from had somehow snapped. The string was still hanging loosely round her neck, but the owl had gone.

Toni was on her hands and knees in her bedroom, searching under her bed and under the dressing table. She even climbed under her bed and checked the loose floorboard to see if the owl had mysteriously managed to get in there. Out on the landing Toni continued her search, wondering if the owl had fallen off when she was half way down the stairs.

Little Maureen was watching her, playing with a toy she was holding in her hand.

"What are you looking for?" Maureen asked looking down at Toni.

"I have lost my owl," Toni cried, "It must have fallen off."

"What talk do owls do?" Maureen asked.

"What sound do they make?" Toni wondered, looking up at the girl, "They go Too wit too woo!"

"Too wit too woo, too wit too woo" Maureen sang as she waved her toy in the air.

Toni glanced up.

"What have you got there Maureen?"

"It's mine, too wit too woo, too wit too woo."

"Can I see it please?" Toni asked, wondering what it could be.

"No! Shan't its mine!" Maureen ran off shouting 'Too wit too woo' all the way downstairs to the kitchen.

Toni got up and ran after her.

"Maureen, have you found my owl for me?" Toni asked kindly.

"It's mine, it's mine, it's mine, I founded it first!"

Toni was chasing after Maureen round and round the kitchen. Maureen stopped and threw something into the fireplace. Toni was horrified, a few wisps of smoke and a crackle of flames had just begun to flicker in the hearth where Edna had been lighting their fire.

"My owl! She has flung my owl into the flames!"

Tom was there in an instant. With the help of a long poker and a brass coal shovel he managed to rescue the owl, but not before the edge of the ancient object had been badly singed and blackened. Tom helped Toni to clean her precious owl and thread the leather string through it. The chord round her neck was now a shorter, but Tom was sure the owl would be safe now.

Toni was distressed and could hardly smile but little Maureen did not realise what she had done; she had run back upstairs to see if she could find something else to play with. She liked playing with Toni, especially when she was chasing after her.

*

Dr Roberts owned the only car in the village. It was apparently a 'Ford Model B,' according to one of the local boys. Toni remembered seeing one before, when an aunt of hers had been taken to church for her wedding. It was a car just like the doctor's one, only the wedding car had been painted white.

There was a loud clatter outside which announced Dr Robert's arrival. Toni walked out to see quite a large crowd of well wishers had assembled in the street to see her off.

Tom and his wife Edna were standing together; they were ready to say good bye.

"We will never forget you Toni," Tom said, "You did something very important for our family, we will never be able to thank you enough!"

Toni hugged them both then turned quickly to get in the car. She hated saying long lingering good-byes.

Dr Roberts opened the door for her and insisted she sat in the rear. Toni smiled, feeling just like the queen. She even waved 'royally' as the car began its steady progress towards Tuther.

Toni turned round in her seat to watch Tom and Edna standing in the middle of the road, holding onto their children's hands. Toni waved furiously as the figures gradually became tiny dots in the distance.

"This is kind of you, Dr Roberts." Toni said, "I was not looking forward to catching the bus into Tuther at six in the morning."

"It is my pleasure Toni. I wanted to tell you, I have begun to investigate this CPR you told me about. I have even managed to find some references in an American medical journal. I want to try and get hold of it.

If only you had access to the Internet, Toni thought, *life would be so much easier for you.*

Much to Toni's surprise, even more well-wishers were waiting at the station for her.

"The train you want leaves from platform two," Dr Robert's explained, "It is already 8:40, it will be here any minute now don't be late!"

"That's the train that goes to Reading without stopping isn't it?" Toni asked.

"That's right!" Dr Roberts had a look at his watch again, "You haven't got time to stand here talking about it."

If I get the 8:45 train, then I will not be able to get off at Ulverton and meet up with Miss Booth. Toni tried to walk as slowly as she could, but everyone was hurrying her along so she did not miss the train.

Toni stopped suddenly and grabbed at her stomach.

"I am so sorry. All the excitement of this morning and the car journey in has shaken me up inside." Heads turned wondering what she was talking about.

"I need to go!" Toni ran off in the direction of the nearest ladies toilets, hoping she could stay in there and manage to miss the train when it came in.

From inside her cubicle Toni could hear the sound of the steam train as it rumbled into the station. A hand banged on the door.

"Hurry up Toni! The train won't wait!"

Toni waited an extra few minutes before she finally emerged. The train had thankfully gone on its way without her.

"I tried to get the guard to wait for you," Dr Roberts was saying, "But the stupid man just wouldn't listen to a word I was saying!"

Toni told him it didn't really matter, there was another train to Reading fairly soon.

While they were waiting, Toni was taken into the waiting room where hot cups of tea were being served to passengers by the 'WVS.' There were a few men in uniform travelling back to their units after from a spell of leave at home.

Soon, a few of the well wishers that had been there to see Toni off made their excuses, and began to drift away. In the distance Toni could see a figure standing close to one of the pillars that held up the station roof. The figure was trying not to draw any attention to its self but whenever Toni stared in that direction, a hand seemed to be quickly waving towards her.

Chapter Thirty Six
Ulverton

Toni had only ever been on a train once before. It had taken her and her mother to Portsmouth to visit the dock yard. The inside of the train had in many ways been just like the inside of a bus, with rows and rows of seats all the way down the carriage. There were a few seats facing each other around a table and there were spaces where passengers could put their luggage.

The train that eventually came into Tuther station was different. Each carriage was divided up into about five or six compartments, each with its own door. Inside the compartment there were two long bench seats facing each other. Toni thought it was nice to have a room on the train all to herself, but she was not on her own for long. Soon her compartment filled up with quite a few passengers.

Toni stood on the seat to place her parcel on the rack above, then she sat down next to the window so she could wave to her friends as the train left the station. Toni had wanted to leave the window open, but one of the men complained if she did that smoke and smut from the engine would blow inside their carriage making them all cough and sneeze, so Toni let him have his way.

There was hardly room for Toni in the compartment, as a few late comers pushed their way inside. Toni wondered if she would have to give up her seat to them, but there was a guard who made sure no one was standing inside. The adults were all big and they seemed intent upon squashing her right up against the window.

Very soon the train blew its whistle, the guard waved his flag, Toni waved excitedly and they were off on their journey to Reading. It had been a long morning so far. Toni had been got up early after a restless night. She had spent a long time trying to pack and find all she needed, so it was not surprising the gentle rhythm of the rocking train soon began to make her feel sleepy .

Houses, fields, trees and streams slowly slipped by. At first Toni watched through the window, then she rested her head against the vibrating glass and slowly started to nod off to sleep. When the train made its first stop at a station, Toni sat up to read the stations' sign. It wasn't time to get off yet. She had four more stations to go through before she came to Ulverton. However, by the time the train stopped for the second time Toni was soundly asleep. Her head slumped down onto her chest, her arms neatly folded in front of her.

Toni was dreaming. She was back in Almund Primary School but Miss Booth was now the teacher. Miss Booth was having terrible trouble trying to write on the electronic white board with a stick of chalk. The chalk would not work; Miss Booth was getting cross with herself. The children were trying to tell her to use a pen to write on the board but Miss Booth was being stubborn: she wanted to use chalk.

Then the class computer switched on: a picture was projected onto the board. It was a picture of a sack of potatoes. The potatoes were okay but Miss Booth did not want that picture on her board: she wasn't teaching a lesson about spuds. She started to rub the picture off with a big board duster, but it wouldn't work. No matter how hard she tried to rub, the picture just stayed there. Miss Booth was getting more and more cross. She thought the board duster wouldn't work because it needed to be cleaned. She got a ruler out of her desk and started to bang on the surface of the board duster to clean it. Chalk dust filled the air; the children were coughing and spluttering. The air was filled with dust but Miss Booth just kept on banging and banging, the noise getting louder and louder.

Toni woke up with a start, Miss Booth was banging on the window of her carriage with her umbrella; she was shouting something Toni could not hear.

Toni jumped up and grabbed her parcel; she had the carriage door open and was out on the platform, just as the train began to move away from Ulverton station.

"I thought we were going to meet in secret!" Miss Booth was saying.

"I am so sorry!" Toni explained, "It has been a hectic morning, I nearly lost my owl and then they tried to put me on an earlier train to Reading, one that did not stop here. I didn't know what to do, so I went to hide in the toilets."

Miss Booth laughed, "I might have known things would go all wrong, but you had no need to worry, I was at the other end of the platform, keeping an eye open for you all the time."

"I was wondering who it was trying to hide behind a pillar! I saw you trying to wave, but I did not know who it was."

"I did not want anyone who knew me to see me get on the train, so I hid. When you got into your compartment, I got into the one next to you. I think it was a good idea don't you?"

"You didn't trust me to get off at the right station did you?" Toni asked.

"I have been working with children of your age for a long time, I know better than to trust them to do anything right!"

Miss Booth was quite correct and they both burst out laughing.

Miss Booth and Toni walked to the end of the platform together. They watched as the train began to pull away heading for Reading.

"I have just thought of something very funny," Toni said, "My Mum has always said that I was named after someone who did something important for our family."

"That's very nice," Miss Booth was listening.

"But, just before I left Tom was saying that he would never forget me, because of the important thing I did for him."

"He is right, you saved his life, and there cannot be anything more important than that!"

"I know, but don't you see, I must be the first person to ever be named after themselves!"

"Just don't go travelling in time again Toni, it makes life far too complicated!"

They stood still for a moment wondering what to say.

"Have you got your silver necklace with you?" Toni asked.

"Of course I have, I never go anywhere without it!" Miss Booth was smiling, "I know you will have remembered your owl!"

"If I touch your disk with it now, do you think I will find myself lost in the middle of Ulverton?"

"I don't think so; you will probably be back where you started. I have read a few books and stories about travelling in time, none of them really make any sense, but I think the two disks are some sort of 'doors' or 'gateways,' at either end of some type of time tunnel. Your owl is the key that opens it up for you."

Toni carried on walking beside her friend, thinking things over.

"If I touch the disk with my owl, will you come with me too? Will you be carried forward to my time from yours?" Toni took hold of Miss Booth's hand and asked, "Do you want to come with me and live in my time?"

"I would love to come with you, but if I do, then the disk will come with me because it is round my neck. We have to travel to the other end of the tunnel which is of course where my disk will be in the future. If I come with you, we will change history."

Toni nodded. She was trying to make sense of it all. Miss Booth was thinking something else that was important.

"I have to find a way to put the owl under the floorboards for you to find one day. If I do not put it there, then you won't be able to find it. If you cannot find it, you won't ever have it round your neck, so you won't travel here!"

"It's like a big circle," Toni thought, "If the circle of events gets broken in any way, then it's as if the spell is broken."

"I see it like a big circle of dominoes, all standing on end. When one is toppled over, it pushes the next one over and so on, right round the circle," said Miss Booth.

"So Toni, although I would love to come back with you to your future to see what it is like, I must never do so because it would break the chain. I have to stop here and put the owl back."

Toni thought of something else.

"You will find the school log book in my room too! Just tell them I told you where it was. It will give you an excuse to go and look for it upstairs."

For a minute Miss Booth looked shocked.

Toni put her arms around Miss Booth and gave her a huge hug.

"Thank you for helping me to get back to my Mum. Without you it would never have been possible. I will never forget you, Miss Booth."

"I will never forget you either Toni, though I will never know if you actually make it back to your own time."

"But I must get there Miss Booth, how else could I have travelled here to find this owl in the woods? It is all part of the chain. It's why I was named Toni after all. "

Miss Booth took the silver necklace from round her neck and carefully placed it on the floor. Then she stepped back so she would not be caught up in anything Toni did.

After a few deep breaths, Toni stepped forward, holding her owl in her hand. She waved to Miss Booth then gently touched her owl against the silver disk, certain she knew what was going to happen next...

Author's Note

I wanted to write a story that saw the Second World War through the eyes of children. I was born just after the end of the war, in 1951. In my own early childhood I am told there was a little of the rationing of war time, but I was not aware of it.

I therefore sought out stories and memories from those I knew who had lived through the war as children themselves. It is thanks to them the story gradually began to take shape.

My thanks go to Margaret Gilmore, Joan Searle and many other members of the Portchester Community Association who all told me stories about what it had been like for them as children, during the Second World War. My particular thanks goes to Maureen Raven, whose memory of the 'barrage balloons' gave me the title for this story.

The story is based in the imaginary town of Tuther which is not very far from where I now live, near Portsmouth, if that makes any sense. Nuther, Uther, Ulverton and Wether only exist in my own imagination.

I have included two extracts from different sources in this story.

You are my Sunshine: there are two versions of this song

The first was recorded for Bluebird Records (RCA-Victor's budget label) on August 22, 1939 by The Pine Ridge Boys (Marvin Taylor and Doug Spivey).

The second was recorded for Decca Records on September 13, 1939 by The Rice Brothers Gang.

In my story Toni reads, recites and sings songs from 'Old Possum's Book of Practical Cats' by T S Elliot, first published in 1939, by Faber and Faber. These poems were used by Andrew Lloyd Webber in his musical 'Cats' premiered in London's West End in 1981 and on Broadway in 1982, Toni had of course been to see this wonderful musical with her mother!

Toni's adventures in this story are fiction, although they are based on real events. As far as I have been able, I have tried to make sure that this story is historically correct; I may have made a few errors though!

Thanks go to Jean, for trying to find all of my mistakes and to Emily, for listening to the story and making suggestions.

G Kelly

'Elephants in the Sky' is set in Tuther. There are other Tuther stories that are available:

Tilly

Tilly Marchant finds school work impossible. She struggles to read and panics with any kind of maths. When her Uncle Howard buys her a magic set, everything in her life changes. She finally finds something that she can do really well. She enjoys mesmerising her class mates each week with yet another amazing trick. Tilly and her family have to move to a new village. Tilly and her Mum struggle to find a suitable school for her. After visiting many unusual schools they finally stumble upon Mr Mistoffelees Amazing Conjuring School. Tilly is very happy here. She makes a new friend called Lorna. Lorna is different; she can perform a different kind of magic.

Crunchem Hall

When Charlie starts to attend Crunchem Hall Primary School she cannot believe how terrible the school is. All the children are taught together in a large hall. Charlie feels as if she has stepped back in time to an era when education relied on chanting tables and facts.

Discipline is harsh; the head teacher is authoritarian and nasty. Charlie cannot wait to find a way out of the school.

Sally and the Alien Cockroaches:
When Sally moves to a new home she does not realise that a family of alien creatures are living behind a false wall in her bedroom. Sally and Maggs are the only girls in Techno Primary school. Their adventure starts when Sally brings to school a piece of metal that she found in the garden shed.

Are those really diamonds Becky?
Becky comes back from holiday in Amsterdam with a little Dutch doll. The dolls' head accidentally falls off in school and an adventure begins involving a gang of diamond smugglers.

A God Mother called Gordon?
Debbie, a keen gardener, discovers that she is the long lost Princess of Flavalia.
This of course entitles her to have a fairy godmother. However, there is a shortage of fairy Godmothers, so she gets Gordon, who, sadly, is only a 'level one' Godmother. Gordon's only accomplishment so far is to spin round in a circle and shout, "Zing!"
Together Gordon and Debbie set out to restore the kingdom of Flavalia to its former glory. However, they don't realise that Janice has other ideas.

And my Manx Trilogy

These stories are available on Kindle and in paperback.

Iron Pier:
When Denver finally came round, he was lying under a cast iron bed. Outside he could see horses and carts rumbling past. There was a paddle steamer in the harbour. In 2005 Douglas on the Isle of Man did not have an iron pier that stretched out into the bay, but it did now!
Where was he?
How did he get here?
Why was a young Irish girl crying?
And what was he doing under her bed?

The Manxman's Tin Box:
In 1914 the world is in turmoil with war fast approaching. The holiday town of Douglas, Isle of Man, is bursting with visitors eager to grab some sense of normality before the inevitable declaration tears their world apart.
The sparkle of diamonds and flashing eyes lead to a robbery that quickly turns to murder. Edward is trapped with no hope of escape except the chance to enlist and hide in a crowd, sure that it would all be over by Christmas. However, life expectancy at the front line is measured in seconds.
The soldier's tin box lies hidden for many years, its location known only to a casualty of war. Edward's desire to possess the jewel is so strong that it continues - even beyond his grave.

Manannan's Silver Mist:
An ancient Manx legend says that Manannan, an evil wizard, banished all magical, enchanted people to live on the island of Innys Shee.
Then he cast a curse making the island submerge beneath the waves, only to return to the surface for a few hours, once every seven years.
Meave, a young teenager, decides to leave Innys Shee when it next

rises above the water, her parents know that she is facing total destruction.

G. Kelly

*

Made in the USA
Charleston, SC
26 May 2016